THE
CATCHER'S
TRAP

THE
CATCHER'S
TRAP

RICARDO HENRIQUEZ

INKSHARES

Published by Inkshares, Inc., San Francisco, California
www.inkshares.com

Edited and designed by Girl Friday Productions
www.girlfridayproductions.com

Cover design by Marc Cohen
Cover image © hikrcn/Shutterstock
Cover image © Igor Zh./Shutterstock

ISBN: 9781942645047
e-ISBN: 9781942645054
Library of Congress Control Number: 2016931683

First edition

Printed in the United States of America

To Tom, for holding my hand and my shield during the time of demons.

PART ONE

THE DOOR TO HELL

CHAPTER 1

The door to hell stands under a fluorescent light in an alley in Queens. The devil himself showed me.

***

I didn't hear any music coming from the building. Nobody was smoking outside, and no other partygoers had arrived, just Roman, his friends Raine and Norhan, and me. The situation had all the elements of a *CSI* episode, and I'd be playing the part of Corpse Number One.

I knew that leaving a bar with a group of strangers was a terrible idea, but I couldn't say no to Roman. He was like the sound of the ocean at night, intimidating and alluring.

Roman's voice had the power to transform the most mundane actions into epic adventures. But it wasn't only his voice. It was the vivid way he described things, the over-the-top adjectives and random historical references. His words could turn a forty-five-minute trip on the subway into a quest to Middle-earth.

"Imagine Berlin pre–War World II. Decadence, lust, and fun were all synonyms back then. There was no judgment, just an insatiable appetite for pleasure." His hands were drawing pictures in the air as if sound were not enough to describe the greatness of the party we were about to attend. "You'll love it, Andres. I promise!"

"I don't think I am down for an orgy." I laughed nervously.

"If you don't like it, you can just get dressed and leave." Roman winked at me.

Maybe that's why I decided to stay. How could a loser like me say no to such promises? The wave of putrid sweetness from the Dumpsters was a warning sign, but I ignored it. I wanted to see Roman's utopia and become part of one of his stories.

The heat rising from the door handle woke my cold fingers. The tingling sensation climbed my arm like a snake. It wasn't an electric shock. It was a different kind of energy. It wasn't painful, just unnerving.

I yanked my hand off the handle and took a step back. A black aura clouded my vision while that numbing sensation I felt every time I got up too fast paralyzed me for a couple of seconds.

"Everything all right, Andres?" Raine said while she lit another cigarette, the third one in the last half hour.

I tried to sound casual. "Something is going on with the handle."

She leaned against the wall and smirked. The fluorescent lighting accentuated the wide pores peeking from under a thick layer of makeup.

"I can get the door for you if it is too heavy," she said, speaking in that condescending baby voice adults use to talk to children.

She was a bitch and not pretty enough to get away with it. I grabbed the handle again, but this time, it was nothing but a cold piece of metal, just a little sticky from the many who had opened it in the past hours.

There is nothing wrong with the door. It is just my anxiety, I thought while taking a deep breath.

I was not much of a party guy. I was always the one who stood in a corner, looking at his phone while others drank, laughed, and became Facebook friends. I tried to mingle. I attempted to make friends, and every once in a while, I even tried to get laid. I just didn't have the talent for it.

"So why am I here?" I said to myself.

I racked my brain for an answer that made sense and had no choice but to admit, despite all the lies I kept telling myself, I wished I had a regular life. I wanted friends, dinner plans, and random hookups. I wanted to meet the love of my life and break up with her two months later when she started talking about meeting her family. That was the reason I went out that night. That was the reason I followed Roman.

"Andres, if you'd rather go home, that's cool." Roman looked at me with an annoyed expression. He had heard me talking to myself.

"I'm fine," I lied while I pulled the door open.

I felt his hand on my shoulder—his grip solid and unbending. I tried to turn around, but he kept me looking straight ahead and moving forward.

"There is no turning back, my friend. Now you walk in there and have fun, doctor's orders." His voice was friendly but firm, and part of me was thankful he was taking charge and stopping me from running away.

Walking through the door felt like stepping into a tunnel. Darkness engulfed us for at least thirty seconds until light and sound became real again. In front of my scared eyes, bodies covered in glittering sweat bathed in an ocean of white smoke. The steam emanating from the walls smelled like myrrh—the incense scent of choice of my childhood church. I took off my denim jacket, trying to ease the sensation of walking into a bowl of hot soup. After two seconds, I was already dripping with regret.

"You can do better than that," Raine said in my ear, pointing at my jacket and pouting her lips toward my shirt.

Without a second thought, she took her shirt off. Her bra sparkled with tiny crystal flowers embroidered on red lace. Her breasts were too small for her athletic frame. They seemed misplaced, as if they were the product of a splicing experiment gone wrong. The pale skin on her arms concealed hills of defined muscles strong enough to take on any man.

"Remember . . . clothing is optional," she purred.

I knew she wasn't flirting with me. On the contrary, she was mocking me, showing me what a joke she thought I was.

The thick air entered my lungs and remained there like a heavy meal. I found myself gasping for a second, but the more I inhaled, the more I started craving the sweet smell surrounding me.

Maybe it was the smoke, the smells, or the lights, but I could tell there was something staged about the place. It wasn't just a party; it was the most outrageous party I had ever seen, and I knew someone had worked hard to make us believe that mirage was real.

The music hit my forehead with the strength of a sledgehammer. Monotonous lyrics on a loop, wrapped in screeching metallic sounds bounced from wall to wall and landed like javelins in my eardrums. It was just arrhythmic sounds with enchanting power, and the crowd loved it.

"So what you think?" Roman yelled over the unrecognizable song.

"It's cool," I lied.

"Give it a minute, you'll like it."

We marched into the shapeless, unsynchronized human mass bouncing in front of us. There was no path to follow; we had to use our bodies like machetes and create a trail to cross the writhing jungle.

On the dance floor, a group of girls were performing their mating dances like nymphs around a campfire. They slowed their movements as if it were Pan, the son of Hermes, who was whispering in their ears and not a car-factory-inspired electronic band. Their hands were reaching for the ceiling while their hips moved from side to side, their mouths half-open, waiting for rain to fall from the sky and mitigate their thirst. It was carnal and mesmerizing. I couldn't help but stare and wonder why their efforts were going unnoticed—why no guys were standing close to them or even looking at them.

"Easy prey. We can attack later if you want," Roman whispered in my ear while pointing at the women dancing.

I nodded and kept walking. There was something unsettling in the way he looked at them. Somehow the word *attack* didn't sound like a figure of speech. Behind Roman's kind face there was a dark presence, a wild animal waiting for the right moment to come out and feed.

We moved toward the bar, rubbing against bodies. I let strangers put their sweaty hands on my chest and grab my ass without consequences. I smiled at chicks with eyes too big for their faces and thanked guys who told me I was cute.

Roman was still behind me, but his friends had vanished.

"This is a little too packed for me," I yelled over my shoulder.

Roman ignored me.

Deeper into the belly of the party, I noticed a group of giant men roaming the room. Their noses were pointing up like bloodhounds following a scent. Their massive arms were covered in crimson scars, and their wide chests were like mountain ranges. There was something strange about their faces—maybe an odd shape around their eyes—but it was hard to see in the dim and distorted light.

One of the giants grabbed a man taking pictures with his phone and dragged him out like a rag doll. The man's eyes were wide and watery. He was screaming for help, his feet kicking the floor as he attempted to stop his captor. Nobody seemed to notice or care.

I wanted to run in the opposite direction, but I had promised myself I would step out of my comfort zone and try to have fun.

"You need strong security when you have so many people in one place," said Roman as if he could read my mind. "I know these guys. They look scary, but if you are not an idiot, they are cool." His words didn't make my anxiety go away.

"What's up with those scars?" I yelled.

"Medals of Honor." His answer made no sense.

The party was not my scene, but then again, what was my scene? I had no friends, and I almost never went out. I was not even a nerd or a geek, which would have, at least, given me a tribe or a purpose. I was just a socially awkward, bland guy. My mom would have slapped me if she knew I was describing myself that way, but it was the truth.

"You are a loving, smart, and good-looking kid! Stop being so negative!" my mother said every time she had a chance. She was my biggest fan. But at the end of the day, that was her duty. Cheerleading for the runt of the litter was in her job description.

The thought of her kept me walking. She wouldn't approve of this place, but she would be happy to see me making friends. A miracle had occurred earlier; a group of "cool kids" invited me to a party, and it wasn't part of a mean joke or an attempted robbery. I ignored the bubbling angst rising from my gut, wiped my wet palms on my jeans, and pushed forward.

"A drink will make me feel better," I said to myself.

We were almost at the bar when a man with blue rings all over his torso stepped in front of me. I wondered why all the weirdoes walked around shirtless.

His eyes scrutinized me like a child looking at a zoo animal for the first time. There was something peculiar in the shape of his face. He reminded me of a Picasso I saw at the Met, unsettling but intriguing and attractive in a weird way.

His breath smelled like licorice. The scent coming out of his mouth was candy-store strong. There was something unevolved about him, as if he had skipped a step or two on his way to becoming a *Homo sapiens*.

The tattoos on his chest were circular saw blades. There was a tribal flair to them, something that felt ceremonial. Even though I didn't understand their meaning, they seemed familiar.

I tried to pass him, but he blocked my way and continued to stare, tilting his head from side to side, studying me and assessing me like I was an object he wanted to purchase. The situation was crossing the line from weird into seriously creepy.

I said hi and waved my palm in front of his eyes. He hadn't blinked at all for the whole minute he'd been standing in front of me.

He wet his lips, smiled, mumbled something that sounded like "walker" and grabbed my hand.

"Dude, that wasn't an invitation! I'm not . . ." His grip hurt, and the more I tried to free myself, the harder he crushed my hand. He wasn't even looking at me, just dragging me with the gravitational strength of a black hole.

The crowd opened in front of him like the Red Sea, and he started walking with me struggling behind. I turned my head around, begging for help, but Roman was nowhere to be found.

"Let me go, asshole!"

The music muted my screams. I knew he couldn't hear me. Nobody could hear me. I looked around with pleading eyes, but I was alone, surrounded by people but ignored by the rest of world.

My foot hit his leg with all the force I could muster, one, two, three times. He turned around and spoke for the first time.

"Stop that. We need to get out," he said, moving his lips slow so I could read them.

"Come on, dude, this is not funny," I said, my voice shaking.

He stopped and got close to my ear. He didn't let go of my hand.

"I don't know how you ended up here, walker, but I need to get you out," he said with a slight shake in his voice.

He started dragging me again. For only one second I wondered why he was calling me "walker," but the urgency to free myself was more important than whatever name he wanted to give me.

I screamed at the top of my lungs, cursing him and kicking him, but he was undisturbed. His legs were thick as the walls of a dam. Every time my foot slammed against him, my entire body trembled. He continued walking, oblivious to my attacks.

I couldn't feel my fingers. My legs ached, and my eyes filled with tears. I felt numb, weak.

"Please don't pass out, please don't pass out." The words fell from my lips like a mantra. I knew that if my nerves got the best of me and I blacked out, I had no chance of leaving the party in one piece.

Roman walked past me and got in front of the guy. His eyes were blazing pits of fire. There was something lethal in his stare, and the guy saw it and took a step backward—his hand still locked into mine. They started arguing. I didn't know how they could hear each other, but it was clear an intense exchange was taking place. The man pushed Roman to the side, but Roman didn't move an inch.

Roman shoved the man, sending him stumbling back. My captor's hand let go of mine and rose in the form of a fist launching toward Roman's face. The crowd opened up, creating a ring for the match.

Raine appeared next to me, giggling like a little girl watching two puppies play.

"When was the last time two studs fought for you, sweetheart?"

Blood rushed to my face, and I looked down. She was right. I was standing there like a damsel in distress, letting a knight in a shiny tank top save me.

Roman received the blow like a professional boxer. He took a couple of steps back and then charged the guy with the might of a rampaging bull. They both fell to the ground, entangled in a knot of fists and rage.

Roman grabbed the guy by his throat and started squeezing, unbothered by the punches raining over him. The tattooed man began losing strength, and before he knew it, Roman was on top of him, pounding his face until blood started gushing. I thought he was going to kill him when two of the bouncers appeared.

Roman got up, ran his fingers through his hair, and spit words that seemed like orders. Without a second thought, the giants dragged the unconscious man away.

That should have been my cue to get out of that noisy and foggy asylum. I should have thanked Roman and headed home. I had tried to do something different and exciting, and I had failed. It was time to go, but instead, against every screaming sense in my body, I stayed.

I couldn't understand my actions. There was a force anchoring me to that place. I was terrified, and at the same time, I wanted to see what other surprises were waiting for me.

"Thank you," I said to Roman as we walked toward the bar.

"That could have ended badly. What about you throw a punch next time someone tries to kidnap you?" Roman yelled in my ear.

I was too mortified to reply.

The scene at the bar was weirdly normal. If it weren't for the fact that I almost got kidnapped by a direct descendant of the missing link, who was later dragged away by two giants, I would have thought that this was a regular bar in Midtown Manhattan.

"What are you drinking?" Roman asked me while leaning on an open space between a guy and a girl who were flirting with each other. The guy gave him a look and mumbled, "Douche."

"Beer, a Stella," I said, and he smiled. We had known each other for just a couple of hours, and we already had an inside joke.

My tongue felt like a dry sponge sitting in my mouth. My shirt was damp, and my lips were eager to taste that beer.

"Take your shirt off if you are too hot." Roman pointed to the flock of shirtless guys walking around.

"I'm fine, just need a beer," I said a little bit more brusquely than I intended. Roman took his tank top off and threw it on the floor.

"It got blood on it," he said, unaware of how unsettling the comment was.

He was tall and lean, his face shaped in sharp edges aligned in a symmetrical way that seemed man-made. He wasn't good-looking in a traditional way; his cheekbones were too high, his chin was too square, and his eyes were too close together, but somehow it worked for him. I wasn't ready to say the words out loud, but I was attracted to him. Roman sparked in me feelings I had fought against my whole life.

"Why did you invite me to the party?"

"I don't know, you seemed cool." Roman's gaze was wandering.

"I don't think many people would describe me as cool."

"I don't care about what others have to say. Believe it or not, Andres, you are special."

His eyes jumped from face to face, scanning for something or someone. I assumed he was thinking of an excuse to leave; after all, I had been nothing but trouble so far, and a guy like him could get laid with a lot less effort.

He fixated on an older guy on the other side of the room. A big smile bloomed on his face. He turned to look at me, cupped my face with both hands, and said, "Just wait here, you're going to love this."

The hungry mob piling on the dance floor swallowed Roman's body. His scent lingered like a dense fog on a winter morning. I could taste black pepper and limes. There was also something salty and spicy, like the aromas of a foreign market next to the sea. Then it was gone, and the odor of hundreds of human bodies grinding in the gloom of the warehouse was all I could smell.

The spell holding me hostage in the party left too. I needed to go home, not only because of the uneasiness I felt since the moment I entered the building, but because I knew what Roman wanted, and I knew I didn't have the strength to say no.

The idea of crossing alone the nine circles of hell I had just survived went against every ounce of common sense I had.

I went to check the time when I noticed my phone was missing. Either it had fallen from my pocket while I'd struggled with the tattooed weirdo or someone had stolen it. That last thought simmered in my mind for a minute. The image of Raine whispering in my ear during the fight replayed in my head, and the pieces fell into place like the ending of an M. Night Shyamalan movie. She took the phone. I had no proof, but I knew it.

I felt eyes drilling my skull, the heavy weight of stares pushing down on my shoulders and chilling my spine. It wasn't my imagination. From all corners of the bar, people were watching me. Men and women from urban tribes I had never encountered before were staring me as if I were a dish they were dying to devour but knew they could not touch.

I locked eyes with a young kid in the middle of the bar; it was obvious he was not old enough to be drinking. Next to him, a tall and attractive woman with skin the color of pearls and long red hair was whispering something in his ear. He looked familiar, but I couldn't remember where I had met him before. He mumbled something, maybe to himself, maybe to me, I couldn't tell. I kept watching him, trying to solve the puzzle he was reciting, and then I got it: he was praying.

I noticed the woman's left hand was on his shoulder. A red stain was forming where her black nails dug into his white T-shirt. She didn't seem to notice the blood running down his young arm, or she just didn't care. Those around them didn't see it either. Their eyes were too distracted by her witchy beauty.

"She is not human," I said.

It was absurd, but I couldn't get rid of the thought. My eyes leaped from one face to another, and despite my brain's efforts to fit the picture within the boundaries of my reality, I couldn't deny that something strange was brewing around me. I saw one of the giants grabbing another man, and then it became apparent; there were two types of creatures in this place: predators and cattle. I had been brought there as the latter.

It was ridiculous—I knew that—but I felt the urgency of escaping before half of the party turned into man-eating monsters.

"You are acting insane," I said out loud, but this time, insanity was winning.

My breathing was short and fast. Cold drops of sweat were running down my forehead. A panic attack was on the horizon like a tidal wave menacing the beach where I stood. My knees felt weak and my skin numb.

"Get your shit together, Andres!" I scolded myself as if my rough inner voice would scare the fear away.

I started walking toward a wall just past the bar. My survival instinct had taken over, and it was guiding my body without waiting for my permission. If I followed the wall, I could make it to the exit door. I thought this was safer than venturing into the core of Hades for the second time.

I was a pathetic idiot. Roman could have invited me to pet a puppy in his house or offered me candy out of his windowless van, and I would have fallen for it. My weakness had nothing to do with his charm and everything to do with my loneliness. Roman had smelled my desperation and preyed upon it.

I hated myself more than usual, but I knew I had to snap out of that puddle of shame and keep pushing. It wasn't too late. I just had to walk until I found the exit, and I would be ok. From there it was just running to the closest subway station.

I followed the outline of the wall for a long time. The edges of the concrete and metal vault holding us hostage were as crowded as the middle of the dance floor. My shoes stuck to the ground with every step. The moisture in the air was becoming molasses on the floor; the sweet flavor I had tasted at the beginning had become sour. The place was decaying, rotting in plain sight, but the bleary eyes of the damned couldn't see it.

The logical part of my brain was losing the battle against the wrenching gut feeling that I had walked through a portal to hell. Even though I grew up in a house where the existence of the devil was considered a fact and diabolical possession a thing that happened even to the best families, I never believed in the supernatural. For the women in my family, ghosts, spirits, witches, and saints were as real as the churches where they prayed every Sunday and as influential in our destinies as the men and women ruling the country.

I was raised around rituals of cleansing, afternoons of praying, and hours of imploring guidance from the dead. Grandma Elisa had countless streams of cautionary tales about men and women falling for the allures of the evil one.

"The devil doesn't have horns or a tail. That's just a story to scare children. The devil is handsome, charming, and quite nice." My grandma's words echoed in my head. "But you can beat him, Andres, *tu estás bendecido, mijo.*" But at that moment, I didn't feel blessed at all.

Maybe Roman had put something in my beer, which would explain the panic, the distorted faces, and the nightmarish creatures I could feel lurking in my blind spot. Something was clouding my judgment, handicapping my senses, making me see and feel things that were not there.

A mindless dancer blocked my way, forcing me to let go of the wall. That was all it took for the human current to grab me and take me away. I bounced, spun, and gasped for air like a drowning victim mangled by raging waves. I knew the feeling. I had experienced it when I was thirteen, and I thought that making it to the swimming team made me immune to the capricious will of the ocean. Back then, a fishing boat had saved me; this time, I had to save myself.

I got my initial panic under control and let my body drift, waiting for the tide to slow down.

"Just don't fall. Let them mangle you, but don't lose your footing," I told myself.

I was dragged to the eye of the hurricane, a spot that seemed protected by an invisible force field. I could see the chaotic mass still rolling around me, but somehow I was safe; nobody was bumping into me or grabbing me. I felt a second of relief, but it went away soon. I couldn't see the wall or any sign of the exit.

It had to be past 2:00 a.m., and the party didn't show any signs of slowing down. I fought the surge of exhaustion taking over my limbs. I had to keep moving. I didn't know what kind of danger I was in, but I knew the stakes were high.

I held my breath and pushed my way through the crowd. The only way to get out of that place was to keep on moving.

Just a couple of feet later, I bumped into the only other human being not dancing in the whole place. She was standing idle, looking in all directions with the same lost expression I was wearing. She was looking for a way out, and that gave me a sense of relief. I had found an ally.

"Hi, are you looking for the exit door too?" I said, getting closer to her.

She turned around and looked at me with so much fear I felt like hugging her. Tiny blood rivers crossed the white part of her eyes. The makeup from her eyelashes was splattered over her cheeks as if her stylist were Jackson Pollock.

Her face was long and angular, her lips thin and wide, and her eyes big like a Margaret Keane model. Her frame was so small she looked like a child, but she was an adult woman, probably in her late twenties.

"There is no exit," she spoke in my ear.

Distress and hopelessness covered the trembling in her voice. Her gaze swung from side to side as she waited for someone or something to jump from the shadows. I didn't understand what she meant. Were there people guarding the doors, preventing others from leaving?

"What do you mean there is no exit?" I yelled over the noise.

"There is no way out. I walked for hours, and the entrance is gone."

She waited for my response, but I didn't know what to say. Doors couldn't just disappear; also, who would take hundreds of people hostage and think they could get away with it? No matter how drunk or messed up the crowd was, when they realized this was a trap, they would rebel and fight back.

"We can find the way out together. I'll get you home safe." I grabbed her hand and started moving, but she didn't follow me, she stood there like a stone figure.

A warm tenderness emanated from her grip. It was in the way she positioned her fingers, in the way she squeezed my palm like we were sharing a painful good-bye. She was done fighting. I could see it in her expression of excruciating loss. I recognized the look in her eyes. She pitied me.

"We are never going home. You don't get it." Tears started rolling from her eyes.

"What's your name?" I asked, trying to calm her down.

"It doesn't matter." She kept looking left and right. She was scared.

"I'm Andres. Who brought you here?"

"She is coming for me."

"Who?"

"The catcher," she said haltingly.

Her mouth opened, but no words came out. Her expression distorted into a mask of horror, her eyes dead and her body shaking. She saw something I didn't. I looked in all directions, but the boogeyman haunting her was not there. I clutched both of her hands and looked into her eyes. Her pupils had almost erased her irises.

I pushed her to walk, but she wouldn't. Her body was petrified while her mind was traveling through a hell I couldn't see.

"I can take it from here," a woman's voice said on my right side.

Her skin was like dead leaves, and her features reminded me of a rat. Her black hair was slicked back, hugging her skull like a shiny leather globe. Her eyes held the intensity of a sociopath, and her posture reminded me of a mantis. She exuded danger.

"I think she needs fresh air; let's take her out." It was a poor attempt, but I had to try.

"I said I'll take it from here. Let her go," she threatened.

"Where are you taking her?"

"Don't you worry. She'll be taken care of." It was the last chance she was giving me.

I let the woman's hands go. Her eyes begged me to rescue her, but I knew I couldn't. Her feet took small and clumsy steps. She looked like a lamb walking into a slaughterhouse. "You don't even know her name," I said as I rushed in the opposite direction.

I pushed my way through the multitude on a path I hoped would take me to the entrance. I saw the heads of the giants floating like magic orbs, scanning the place with their sharp eyes. I tried to stay calm and changed direction every time one of them got too close. I knew they were not looking for me, but their proximity would be a serious threat to my getaway plan.

I continued pressing the slithering bodies, not paying attention to the figures touching me on the way. Men and women would grab my face and my hips, inviting me to stay and join them in their rites of drunken lust. I kept moving, freeing myself from arms like vines in a jungle.

"How big is this place?" I asked, exhausted.

I had walked for what felt like hours without finding a new wall. The only logical explanation was that I was walking in circles. My feet felt like concrete slabs, and the ache from hours of standing made it hard to continue.

The nymphs I had seen when we arrived appeared like an oasis in front of me, their arms still pointing to God and their mouths waiting for manna to feed their hunger. A rush of hope made me smile. I had a north. I knew the entrance was close to them. It was the final stretch.

Without any warning, the music stopped, and the lights went on with a loud sound of snapping switches. At first, the crowd looked confused, but then they started booing. Whistling and yelling replaced the music that had pounded our ears through the night. The growing murmur of a riot rose.

A strong hand grabbed my arm.

"Let's get out of here. This is going to get ugly." Roman's voice took me by surprise.

Raine and Norhan were next to him. His fingers were firm on my skin and showed no sign of letting go. I tried to free myself, but he pulled me along.

"You dropped your phone. Raine found it at the bar." He put the device in my hand.

"Roman, stop! I am not going anywhere with you."

"Don't be an idiot, Andres, this place is a time bomb."

"I have to go home."

"Well, standing there, I doubt you'll make it anytime soon."

We were not walking in the direction of the exit. We were heading toward a black door to the right. Roman turned around and gave me a puzzled look.

"What is wrong with you, man? Did you take something?"

The events of the night were spinning in my head like swirling water. I looked around, and there were no monsters. Just upset partygoers demanding to continue their orgy. Roman was right; the temperature of the place was rising, and there were not enough bouncers to contain the uproar.

Raine and Norhan were right behind me. Their steps were getting so close to mine that I had no choice but to keep moving. Their expressions were devoid of any emotion, and their pace was steady. Even if I tried to escape, there was no way I could outrun those three. They were escorting me, I didn't know where, but Roman's act couldn't fool me; I knew I was not going home.

"Where are you taking me?"

"Somewhere safe," he said matter-of-factly.

"Why?"

"Andres, I get it, you don't make a lot of friends, but this is getting annoying. We have been nothing but nice to you. I left you for two seconds at the bar, and then you were gone. I find you two hours later, and you are acting like this is a scene from *Logan's Run*." He wasn't even looking at me, just marching ahead.

I heard the sound of knuckles colliding with bones and the first howling of the enraged mob. It was starting. Panicked soles hit the floor like a herd of antelope chased by lions. It was mayhem. I looked back at the entrance, and the door was infested with people fighting to leave.

Roman started running, and I followed. The black door was just feet away, and its proximity felt like my salvation.

We rushed into the next room like a band of fugitives. I was so scared and out of breath that I barely noticed the man standing in front of me, offering me a glass of a bubbling liquor. I looked around in awe. The room where I was standing didn't belong to the back of a club, but to a medieval castle. Or a Medieval Times restaurant.

The man continued to stare at me, waving the effervescent liquid in front of my eyes. He was a short, chubby guy with hands so big they looked like tennis rackets. His skin was white and smooth in an unnatural way that gave it the appearance of salt crystals. His hair was a rebellious salt-and-pepper cluster of curls falling all the way to his shoulders. His smile was forced and uncomfortable. The type of tight-teeth grin rich people give to their servants when their friends are around.

"I am Ash. Nice to meet you, Andres," he said, introducing himself. "Roman can't stop talking about you." His handshake reminded me of the slugs I used to play with when I was a child.

The cruelty in his eyes was so palpable I felt like I could see his sins staring back at me. I didn't need to be a mind reader to know he found pleasure in violence. That sixth sense that all humans possess, the inexplicable voice in our heads that tells us to run when danger approaches, started screaming at me as soon as I saw him.

I wasn't sure what to say. The edges of reality were tearing at the seams, and I was holding on to the running pieces of thread. There was only one thing I was sure of; my next move was my last chance to go home.

"Nice to meet you too. I'm sorry to be rude, but I am not feeling well. Is there another way out? I need to go home." I tried to sound as calm and as polite as I could. I knew that asking to leave was the most naive approach, but it was a starting point.

"Of course, but first have a drink with my wife, Embla, and me." Ash pointed to a woman lying down on a green sofa.

Embla looked unconscious. I couldn't imagine how she would even hold a glass, never mind drink. Her skirt was almost all the way up to her waist. Her hair was muddled and her top removed. She looked like the victim of a violent assault.

There were no other doors in the room. Bucolic paintings of landscapes and families in the countryside covered every inch of the walls. There were so many of them of all sizes, hanging from ground to ceiling.

The stone floor felt uneven as I switched my weight from one leg to the other. I didn't have a plan B. I was trapped.

"I shouldn't drink any more. Seriously, I don't want to get sick here." I touched my stomach and made an exaggerated expression of pain.

Roman was standing right behind me, Raine and Norhan flanking him like two trained Dobermans waiting to be released. I thought about my brothers. They would have fought their way out. "Live with honor or die with glory!" Their war cries would have resounded in every corner while they charged their captors and even died in their attempt at freedom. I wasn't ready to die, so I resigned myself to whatever Roman and his friends had planned for me.

"You look so tense, so afraid. Nothing is going to happen to you in this room, Andres. Trust me." Ash's voice was slow and affected. He was putting on a performance. He wanted to be the mustache-twirling villain, the one who tells you his plan as he is about to kill you.

I turned around and looked at Roman, his face blank like a virgin canvas, his eyes concealed with a varnish of indifference.

"Please," I pleaded, almost crying.

"You are being rude, Andres." His voice sounded like a judge reading a sentence.

Ash pulled my shoulder and turned me around. I saw his left arm rise and then go down with fury, letting the back of his hand land on my face like a cannonball. The strike sent me flying across the room. I hit the wall with savage force. My ears were ringing, my eyes blurry. I heard Ash's voice distorted and distant.

"I will enjoy this one."

As a black mist fell in front of my eyes, I thought of that morning, the familiar noises of my neighborhood and that small pill that had promised me salvation.

CHAPTER 2

Hysterical laughs mixed with loud engines and the sound of skateboard wheels hitting the pavement created a junglelike clatter at the entrance of the Queens Center. My neighborhood was not the ideal place for those with a phobia of sensory overload. For sure, it wasn't the perfect place for me, but even though there were days when just walking home from the subway gave me a headache, I liked living there.

I rushed through Queens Boulevard toward the Duane Reade on Fifty-Ninth, begging not to run into anybody. Clueless teenagers stumbling into each other, mothers pushing baby carriages, and distracted McDonald's enthusiasts mesmerized by the golden glitter of their fries turned lunch time in Flushing, New York, into a trying obstacle course.

The strange part of my social anxiety was that this sort of chaos didn't trigger it. I didn't panic, because I was just another anonymous bee. If I eliminated the anticipation of performing any social rituals, walking among faceless human beings was bearable.

I tried to warm my hands in my pockets. I wore a thin blue sweater even though Al Roker said it was "an unusually chilly fall day."

But it was my "good sweater," and I didn't want to cover it with a jacket. What was the point of putting on my only expensive piece of clothing if I had to hide it under a bulky bunch of polyester I bought at JCPenney?

I am not sure why, but I thought the occasion demanded that I dress up. After all, I was on my way to purchase the modern-day soma, the solution to all my problems, a pill so little and so powerful that it would turn my life into a field of ambrosia, or kill me with mass organ failure, according to the side effects listed on its website.

"'All the advantages of Christianity and alcohol, none of their defects,'" I said, quoting Huxley.

The smell of fresh bread from Broadway Bakery mixed with the crisp air of late autumn reminded me of Sundays at home. I missed those days. No soma in the world could bring those days back.

Every Sunday after mass, during the cold months, my grandma would turn off the heat and bake bread.

"You don't need heat *cuando el oven está prendido,*" she would say.

"Elisa, you are freezing us to death!" my mother replied over and over.

To which my grandmother always had the same answer. "Andres needs this, Magali. *El me lo va agradecer*, one day."

It was an odd thing to say, but I assumed Grandma, like everybody else in the family, was coming up with ways to make me stronger, less wimpy, and less embarrassing to the whole clan.

For a while, my mother tried to argue with her, but it was a losing battle. So it became a family tradition: Sundays we wore blankets inside the house.

I often wondered why my mother never thought that I was a lost cause. Even when I gave up on life, she continued pushing me and demanded I dig myself out of the hole of misery where I lived. There were days when I wished she would just throw her arms in the air and walk away. Everybody else did at some point.

"It is called love, Andres; you don't get it, but I do all this because I love you," she said to me.

"Can you love me a little less?"

"Unfortunately, no, *mijo*, I can't."

I reached into my back pocket and made sure the prescription was still there. I ran my fingers over it like it was written in braille, as if my fingertips could read the words on the piece of paper. It said *Lamictal*. I knew that.

The vibration of my phone startled me. I looked at the screen, closed my eyes, and let a flood of dread run all the way to my index finger.

"Hi, Mom," I said, trying to sound cheerful.

"Hi, *mijo*, are you on your way to the pharmacy?"

"Yup, almost there."

An uncomfortable silence followed. I knew what she was feeling. She was happy because there was a glimmer of hope for her damaged child. I never thought the words *endogenous depression* would make someone smile, but for my mother, they were like a Christmas present. At last she had a name for what was wrong with me, and to make things even better, there was a drug that would transform me into what she always dreamed: one of my brothers.

"Andres, don't be embarrassed, it is—"

"Have to go, Mom, I can't hear you. I'll call you later."

I didn't want to listen to her comforting speech. I loved my
mother, but when she went Oprah on me, I couldn't take it.

I would get grief for being rude, but she would get over it;
she loved and pitied me too much to stay mad.

I didn't blame my mother for her disappointment. I wished
I were more like Jorge or Dani, but I didn't have the strength or
will to strive for that kind of excellence. I grew up hearing that
my brothers were heroes, protectors of freedom and democ-
racy fighting on behalf of America in foreign lands. From an
early age, I knew I lacked the discipline and nerve for such
responsibility.

I grew up in a typical Latino family in the East End of
Bridgeport, Connecticut. My father was a Mexican immigrant
who worked all his life in the same restaurant. My mom was a
teacher's assistant at the middle school in the neighborhood
where she grew up.

I was the youngest child and an unexpected addition to the
family. My mom was forty-one when she got pregnant; my dad
was fifty. My father used to say I was a wonderful surprise, not
a "mistake" like my brothers would say, teasing me. My mom
never got involved in those conversations.

I was a shy kid, and that drove my brothers crazy. They saw
my birth as an opportunity for the Campos brothers to leave a
mark on the mean streets of Bridgeport. I was to continue their
legacy and make them proud. But I was far from what people
expected from one of the Camposes. I was quiet, fearful, and
had a tendency to cry often. So they tried to change my DNA
one beating and public humiliation at a time.

Of course, their tactics were a tragic failure. Because of
their constant harassment, I became even more withdrawn. I
hated public events, birthday parties, or any social gathering.
Anything that involved other people was an opportunity for

Jorge and Dani to embarrass me, so I avoided human contact at all costs.

"He is just shy, he'll grow out of it, leave him alone," Mom would say when Jorge called me a pussy or whatever insult he felt was the appropriate one for the occasion.

"He needs to act like a man, Mom. It's for his own good."

Their obsession with my manhood resulted in the most diverse forms of torture. Some weekends—without any warning—they would wake me up before dawn and take me on what they called survival trips. I hated those with a passion. We would spend the day hunting for food, building shelters, and making tools out of the grossest materials.

Jorge and Dani insisted that surviving in the wild was a skill any modern man needed.

"It is a fucked-up world, Brother. You never know when you'll find yourself behind enemy lines," Jorge would say with an ominous voice.

That was when they still thought I would follow the family tradition and become a soldier. By the time I graduated from high school, that dream was dead, buried, and rotting under many layers of disappointments.

When I was a teenager, despite my constant complaints, they became the most tenacious matchmakers.

"You need a girl, Brother. You need to become a man," Dani would say, making the most inappropriate gestures I could imagine.

I never knew what they told the girls they paraded in front of me. But I was sure they were there as an act of charity and not because they thought I was cute.

Dani and Jorge feared I was gay, and so did I. I grew up in a house where the word *gay* was nothing but a euphemism for a mortal sin. But religion was not the engine behind their worry; it was pride. They didn't care about the eternal damnation of my soul. They were terrified of the public humiliation, of admitting that Campos blood was not a synonym of manhood.

I'm from a generation in which bullying was condemned and fourteen-year-olds were celebrated for coming out. But that was not the reality in my house. Maybe because they all suspected I may be gay, my family members went out of their way to express how disgusting they thought the "gay lifestyle" was. They were warning me. Every time my father said, "Those people have no morals," I heard, "Don't you even dare."

By the time I was fifteen, I realized that I was attracted to girls as much as I was attracted to guys, which led my teenage brain to believe that being gay was an option. So I chose to be straight; why make life difficult.

I knew my brothers cared about me. In their narrowed and simplified view of the world, tormenting me was the best medicine for what they thought was some congenital flaw. I didn't hold a grudge; they both lost enough in the war to pay for the sins they committed in their youth.

The pharmacy swarmed with people. At the front register, two cashiers were knocking down a long line of customers while making their best effort not to look over it. I felt their pain. People in stores suck. I had plenty of those experiences at the Whole Foods where I worked, but in that part of town, the customers' undeserved sense of entitlement made the job even harder.

I walked through aisle three toward the pharmacy counter. A path made of Cheerios spread out like the yellow-brick road leading to an empty box lying on the floor. Open containers and milk puddles made the place look like the aftermath of a night of looting. I saw the perpetrators right in front of me.

Two little kids sat down, leaning against a shelf, eating Cheerios from the floor. Their mother was nowhere to be found. I thought of asking them if they were lost, but before I decided if getting involved was worth it, a frantic woman came running like a stampede. Her ponytail bounced like a damaged jack-in-the-box while her high heels hit the floor. It was impossible to determine her age; she was either seventeen or forty-five. Too many cigarettes and a life of struggle had taken a toll on her face.

"People would think I don't feed you at home! Why are you eating shit from the floor?" She slapped the cereal out of the kids' hands and looked at me, expecting me to say something.

"Kids will be kids." The words out my mouth sounded so forced and faked that the woman didn't even bother to respond.

"We like Cheerios," said the smallest child.

She rolled her eyes, huffed, and dragged the two young looters away. She didn't say a word to the kids about trashing the store.

"Dropping off?" The girl at the pharmacy counter flashed her sparkling teeth at me.

She looked familiar. Her green eyes, sprinkled with blue lines, looked like a lagoon we used to visit with my family in Puerto Rico. Her skin was tan and radiant and had a manufactured glow, one of those body lotions with gold drops that Jennifer Lopez promised would turn every girl into a star.

"Yes," I said.

She noticed I was staring.

She took my prescription and typed on her computer with the speed of a sewing machine. Her fingers moved from key to key like ten hungry hummingbirds gorging on a field of wild lilies. She took her eyes away from the screen and looked at me with questioning eyebrows.

"You live in one of those brick buildings on Ninety-Fourth, right? I think we are neighbors."

"I thought you looked familiar," I said, trying to be casual.

Blood was rushing from every corner of my body into my cheeks. A pretty girl was talking to me while holding a prescription for depression medicine. I just needed to be naked for this to sound like the beginning of a recurring nightmare.

I thought maybe she didn't know what kind of medicine I was getting; after all, she wasn't the pharmacist, and there are many pills with similar names.

"Will you wait for your prescription?"

"No, I'll pick it up this evening, thank you."

I knew I should have waited for the medicine and used the opportunity to talk to her, maybe even ask her out, but that was not me. The mere idea of flirting with this girl got me rushing out of the place.

On my way out, I kicked the empty box of Cheerios in aisle three. A man reading the label of a package of cookies gave me a disapproving look; I answered with a smirk.

"If you had my luck, you would be kicking crap too," I felt like barking at him, but I didn't. Instead, I just ran out breathing heavy, hitting the pavement with fury until I was standing in front of my building.

My apartment smelled like the men's locker room at my high school. There were so many piles of dirty clothes spread through the living room that if someone told me Josh's laundry basket had been the target of a terrorist attack, I'd have believed them. I guessed my cousin ran out of clean clothes and raided his laundry looking for a T-shirt that didn't smell like he already wore it for a week straight. He was a pig. But that pig let me live in his apartment for free, so I had no choice but to deal with his pestilence.

"We are blood, dude. You can crash on my couch for as long as you want," he said a couple of months ago when I told him I wanted to move to New York. That was quite generous of him. Of course, charity is never free, and most, if not all, of the cleaning duties landed under my administration as soon as I moved in.

I was picking up Josh's mess, dragging underwear and socks with one foot and holding his shirts with my fingertips, when forty dollars and a condom fell from one of his jeans. My cousin would leave money lying around all the time, but taking into consideration the events of the day, the bounty at my feet felt like an invitation. God was telling me to take that money and that condom, get out of my emo mood, and attempt to have fun.

My phone vibrated again. A text from Josh. *"Not coming home tonight, cousin. Feel free to put the bed to good use! Get some!"* Winking emoji and crying-laughing emoji. The idea of me "getting some" was hysterical to him.

"I will. BTW the house is a mess."

I didn't hear back from him.

These were signs. The girl in the pharmacy, the money, Josh not coming home; the universe threw me a bone. I was going out and forcing myself to enjoy it. I looked at the condom. It had been so long that it looked like an alien object to me. I had to do something about that.

I'd never had a real girlfriend. In college, there was a girl who thought my awkwardness was cute, so she chose me as her go-to booty call. I guess that was the closest I ever got to a relationship. I didn't love her. She was fun to be around, the sex was good enough, and I liked that she didn't mind my inability to hold a conversation. She was not interested in us becoming an item either. As a matter of fact, I am sure she had a boyfriend for most of the time we saw each other.

There were other women here and there and a drunken and unexpected make-out session with David, my college roommate—which both of us decided never to talk about—but nobody who left any everlasting mark.

After I had showered, I stood in front of the mirror, staring at myself. There was a little hill where my abs used to be. It wasn't huge but big enough to stand out from the rest of my body.

"Girls care more about personality than bellies," I said to myself while touching my stomach.

Body insecurity was one of the few personality issues I didn't have. I was a swimmer in high school, so I was in shape most of my teenage years. I never became muscular, but I was lean and had abs I was proud of.

Since I quit the swim team in my senior year, I had not done any other type of physical activity. I didn't have the energy for it. I hated team sports, and the gym in college was always full of idiots. So I would eat trash and watch TV instead.

I put on a loose polo shirt so my stomach would not show. I thought I looked ok. I didn't want to appear desperate, so I went for a relaxed vibe.

I wanted my outfit to say, "I may have a shitty personality, but I have a cute face."

On my way to the subway, I noticed that the madness of the early afternoon had died out. The litter on the sidewalks made it appear as if a parade had passed through the neighborhood, leaving behind a trail of plastic containers, burger wrappers, and brown bags. The air felt empty, the sounds of the wilderness had left the streets, and a daunting silence took its place.

Inside Woodhaven Station, it was just a kid wearing big black headphones on his ears and me. It was forty degrees outside, but he wore shorts and a hoodie. He walked back and forward, bobbing his head to the beat of his music in some ritualistic pattern. There was such intensity in his expression, such commitment to the rhythm shaking his eardrums. I couldn't help but wonder what he was listening to.

I could tell he was angry. The music was his punching bag, and he was hitting it with all his might. Every so often his lips moved, mumbling the lyrics that most reminded him of the source of his ire.

Our eyes locked for a second, and he started walking toward me. He didn't look threatening; on the contrary, he looked sad, a shade of helplessness framed his expression.

"You have a smoke?" he asked.

"Sorry, not a smoker."

"Yeah, I didn't think so, nobody smokes anymore. I should quit too."

Up close he looked even younger, maybe fifteen or sixteen. He wasn't small, though; he was built like a quarterback, but his face gave him away. His red shorts were faded, and his brown hoodie had seen better days, but his headphones looked expensive and brand new.

"Do you have a dollar, then?"

He caught me off guard, and my face showed it.

"I'm not trying to rob you, man. If you don't, that's cool," he said. He looked embarrassed. I imagined asking a stranger for money was not something he often did.

"What's your name?" I asked.

"Lakay. I know . . . it's weird, my parents are weird." The word *parents* had a sour taste; it was obvious and painful to watch. He forced a smile and started walking away.

The subway was full of homeless kids at night, and even more when the temperatures dropped. There were no stores where they could hide and get warm. Lakay was one of those kids, I could tell, but he was different from those I had encountered before. Something told me he wasn't the product of a family struggling with substance abuse or poverty.

"I have a twenty if you want it."

He looked at me with a severe frown. After the words had come out of my mouth, I realized it sounded creepy. A kid had asked me for a dollar, and I had offered him twenty. Of course he had to wonder what I wanted in return.

"That's fine, man. I just wanted a dollar to buy gum," he lied, putting his headphones back on.

Or you can take a twenty and buy yourself a meal, I thought. But it was too late to say it; I had scared him.

The R train arrived just a couple of minutes later. I got in. Lakay didn't.

CHAPTER 3

Tumultuous was the new hot place in Chelsea. The bar still had some of the decor from its time as a gay bar. A signed picture of Bananarama hung at the entrance, a headshot of a young Bea Arthur adorned the top shelf of the bar, and a framed poster from the original production of *The Boy from Oz* marked the door to the men's room. I guess the owner either wanted to respect the history of the building or thought the once-serious mementos were hysterical. Either way, the random items scattered through the place gave it a cool atmosphere.

The light-wood panels and the exposed beams reminded me of a cabin in the mountains. The only thing missing was a big stone fireplace to complete the picture. The name and decor didn't match at all. *Tumultuous* evoked dark corners, graffiti on the walls, and metal columns. Maybe a pool table and benches inked with first names and uninventive drawings. But instead, I was standing in a lounge that could have been transplanted from the Swiss Alps. The more I fixated on the details of the space, the more I felt I would love to meet the schizophrenic mind who birthed it.

Even though the bar area had the proportions of an airport runway, every inch of it was taken. People held to their spots like they were street parking spaces in Midtown. I stood at the far left end, close to the dishwashing area, waiting for an opening. The guy in front of me was a tall businessman-looking dude. I assumed he would find his goal for the night soon and get moving.

I looked at my baggy jeans and plain polo shirt and thought I should have put more thought into my outfit. I got all dressed up to go to the pharmacy but dressed like a middle-aged suburban dad for a night out. I assumed that the crowd would be more laid back on a Thursday night, but I didn't know that there was no "casual" day in Chelsea.

While riding the subway, I decided that trying to get laid was putting too much pressure on myself, so I changed my aim to just talking to a stranger. It sounded pathetic and childish, but I felt it was a fair challenge.

I couldn't remember the last time I had made a friend. Since I left Connecticut, I had lost contact with almost everyone. I didn't have a social-media footprint, so nobody knew what I was up to, and since phone calls became an insulting way of communication for anybody who wasn't a family member over sixty, getting in touch with people was too much of a challenge. My absence in the hallways of Twitter and the crowded galleries of Instagram transformed me into a ghost—a lost soul wandering the purgatory of real life, unaware of the latest Vine celebrity or massive social outrage.

"Reactivate your Facebook, Cousin. It has been so many years since that whole mess. You don't need to be afraid," Josh would say to me.

He was a Facebook celebrity, always posting shirtless pictures and funny statuses. He had friended every girl he ever met, and would meet with several of them on a regular basis.

I was sure that he was staying with one of his Facebook girl-friends that night.

I wasn't afraid of crossing back to the social-media realm. I just didn't want to. I knew that staying offline made it difficult to meet and keep in touch with people, but I didn't care. In that sense I was old-fashioned; I didn't want to fall for someone's thrilling, fake online life just to settle later for the knockoff version that was their reality.

The guy at the bar moved as predicted. There was a blonde with his name written all over her accentuated cleavage.

I ordered a beer, took a deep breath, and got my head in the right space.

Just crack a smile and see what happens, I encouraged myself.

I was almost done with my Coors Light when I noticed another lonely soul. She was standing next to a high table, shifting her eyes from her phone screen to the crowd every ten seconds. I thought maybe she was waiting for someone, but after twenty minutes it became clear that nobody was joining her.

I didn't want to be the kind of guy who targets a girl just because she is alone, but if she was feeling half as lost as I was, she would appreciate the company. Who knew, maybe we were doing the same thing, stepping out of our comfort zones, trying to make friends.

The fifteen feet that separated us were a path of crowded tables rising from the floor like ancient Greek columns. Women in tight outfits and guys with slim suits hovered around tables, holding drinks and displaying rehearsed laughs. There was a theatrical flair to this whole coupling ritual. Everybody knew their lines, everyone had put on this performance before, and they could do it without thinking. I, on the other hand, had the acting skills of a wax figure.

I summoned all my strength and took the plunge. I stood up, straightened my denim jacket, and walked one step at a time, making sure I didn't look too eager or rushed.

Her bob haircut and her bright-red lipstick made her look like a heroine from the thirties. A high-waisted pencil skirt hugged her legs all the way to the bottom of her knees, where a black stripe appeared to frame the whole outfit. The piece of clothing looked uncomfortable and restricted, but she didn't seem bothered. She was wearing a cream-colored blouse made of some shiny material; it could have been silk or satin. There was something sexy about her outfit, even though she looked like Dita Von Teese's Southern Christian cousin.

My beer was almost empty, but the bottle made for a good security blanket, so I didn't let go. I walked a zigzagging line through the tables, hoping the bloody fight between my anxiety and my determination was not showing on my face. At some point, I stopped blinking, afraid that if I closed my eyes, she would vanish.

When I was less than three feet away, she noticed me. Her eyes met mine for a couple of seconds. I could tell she was trying to figure out if she knew me. When her brain search came back empty, she frowned and turned her back to me. It was a clear and loud "get . . . lost."

My face burned. I felt all eyes on me. I heard giggles; I saw girls whispering in each other's ears and men laughing. It was all in my head, of course. Everybody was too busy trying to score their own points to notice how I missed the goal area. My feet started aching, getting ready to run. I had to leave.

"This was dumb," I said out loud and put my beer on a table without looking at who was sitting there. I rushed toward the door, led by anger and frustration.

I was so flustered I almost ran into a man blocking my way. "She's a bitch. She does it all the time, sits there looking desperate and then rejects every guy who approaches her. I think it makes her feel powerful. She is the Mata Hari of Tumultuous, the chick with the Bette Davis eyes." He was talking to me.

His eyes hooked on mine, and his smile shone like a lighthouse in the middle of the stormy sea I was trying to escape.

"Maybe she is just shy," I said, trying to pass him.

"She is quite outgoing when she is in the mood. I've been told." His voice was playful and suggestive.

I smiled.

"I'm Roman. You?"

"Andres," I stuttered while getting my own name out.

Even though my unexpected interaction with Roman felt like a lifesaver, I still wanted to get the hell out of the bar. But he continued to stand there, confident and impressive like a Renaissance sculpture.

"Let me buy you a drink, Andres. Just to show you that not everybody in this bar is an asshole."

"That's ok, I was leaving anyway," I said, but he was already walking toward the bar and didn't hear me, or pretended not to.

I could have turned around and headed to the door. I had just met the guy, so I didn't have to follow him anywhere, but I wanted to. My goal for the night was to meet a stranger, and he was one.

Roman had no problem occupying people's personal space. He wedged his way between patrons and got right in front of the bartender.

In just a matter of seconds, I had a beer in my hands.

"I like Stella," he said. "I know the beer snobs say it is a disgrace to the entire nation of Belgium, but so was King Leopold III's surrender, and nobody seems to bring that up in conversation."

I looked at him, confused, but he continued talking about Belgium's neutrality at the beginning of World War II and their short resistance to the Nazis. Roman could give Google a run for its money when it came to names and dates. He jumped from one period of history to another with the grace of a modern dancer, giving me seconds to catch up with his timeline while I managed monosyllabic answers.

"I bet you are thinking about killing that chick," he said out of nowhere. His smile had a hint of wickedness.

The joke lingered in the air until I found the words to disperse them.

"If I killed every girl who rejected me, I'd be a serial killer."

"Not a bad profession, but not a lucrative career, I've heard," he laughed.

"I don't have much luck with women. I'm kind of used to it," I said, changing the focus from the whole killing-people thing.

"What about guys. I bet guys would love you," he answered in a flirty tone.

Talking to him was fun, but his outpouring waves of charm and smiles made it clear he wanted more than just talking. I didn't know what I wanted. The everyday me wanted to find an excuse and head home. The part of me I hated the most wanted to go home with him. This last thought made me smile. That would be the last shot to kill my brothers' pride.

Roman insisted on having another beer.

"You can't leave yet! It's early. New opportunities may present themselves!"

He started talking about the sorry state of Chelsea. According to him, young families had moved into the neighborhood like hordes of barbarians in the past ten years, turning it into the most boring place in New York. I thought it was still a pretty cool place, but he had strong feelings about it.

"Chelsea was the cradle of film and theater of the East Coast before World War I. A place of secrecy and death during the years of the Manhattan Project. A sex playground for generations of gay men in the eighties. Now it's full of gay couples pushing baby strollers and women carrying yoga mats. It doesn't get much worse than that."

Roman spoke like my grandfather would about the good old days in Puerto Rico, like he had seen the evolution of the neighborhood and not read about it in a *New Yorker* article.

"I am sure you are wondering why am I here, then?" he continued. "Well, the truth is that I like this bar. There is something real about this place. It feels like it hasn't been raped by packs of hipsters yet, but that will change soon, I am sure." He shot words like a tennis-ball launcher, with no breath between sentences.

"Do you come here often?"

"Not often enough," he answered.

There was a brief silence, but it didn't feel uncomfortable. I took a sip of my beer and smiled. Roman was a good-looking guy. He was entertaining and full of stories that ranged from the hysterical to the macabre. His tight white pants and untied black military-style boots made it clear he was not afraid of standing out. He was wearing a white tank top made of some kind of shiny material, which revealed two arms covered in odd-looking tattoos. Screaming faces entangled with demonic-looking creatures were inked right next to fields of flowers growing from what looked like pools of blood.

He was a bad boy who had traveled the world and paid attention in history class; how could anybody not be attracted to him?

"You are not from here, right? You don't look like a New Yorker. New Yorkers are jerks." Roman made a gesture of disgust.

"I'm from Connecticut."

"Never been there," he said, shrugging while checking our surroundings.

"So why do you live here?" I asked.

"I don't."

"Are you on vacation?" The words were flowing.

"Something like that. I am here to pick up stuff for a friend. I am leaving soon."

Roman told me about his friend Ash and how he would travel all over looking for special "pieces" for his collection.

"Lately, he's been on a total American funk. I've been to Chicago, Miami, New York, LA, a total bore. I miss the days when he was obsessed with Turkey. Those trips were just amazing." Roman was talking more to himself than to me.

I started noticing every time his leg leaned against mine, every time he'd pat my arm or grab my shoulder in the middle of one of his stories. Still, I was not completely sure he was hitting on me.

"So are you dating someone, Roman?" I thought the question would open the door to clarify things.

A smile as wide as the Hudson spread through his face. He grabbed my chin with one hand and spoke with a breathless voice: "Is that your pickup line? Well . . . I am all yours, Andres." Then he let my face go with more force than necessary and started laughing.

I managed a half smile and decided it was time to go. He was playing with me, and despite my initial adventurous feelings, I was not ready to open Pandora's box.

Roman sensed my discomfort and with an apologetic look raised his beer, offering me another one.

"I think I should—" I started excusing myself.

"Wait just a minute, Andres. I want to introduce you to my friends."

Raine and Norhan arrived before I could finish my sentence. Norhan greeted me and stood as if he were waiting for instructions. His swollen arms were tensed and ready to strike at the smallest word of encouragement. I noticed his hand's default position was a fist.

"Don't let him scare you, he is a gentle giant," said Raine.

But I wasn't the only one wary about him. Our group was getting looks from every corner of the bar. Norhan had not given anybody a reason to worry. He just minded his own business, drinking his beer and looking distracted. Still, there was an inaudible tick, tock, tick, tock coming from him.

"Why did you come here, Andres? Something tells me bars are not your thing," Roman said, sincerely curious.

I started rambling on about working too much and not leaving time for fun when, as if an oversharing demon had possessed me, I started telling the story of that morning—the kids eating Cheerios in aisle three, my depression, the pretty girl at the pharmacy counter. Before I knew it, I had vomited my entire soul in front of a stranger.

I scanned Roman's face for a sign of boredom or annoyance, but he was looking at me with attention, maybe even sympathy.

Raine and Norhan showed no interest in joining our conversation, but it didn't bother me; they were not the main attraction in this ride. Roman was the ringleader, and he cared, and for some reason, that seemed important to me.

He told me about his own struggle figuring out his place in the world and how at some point he just stopped bothering with other people's opinions.

"An important woman adopted me, and she had plans for me from the moment she held me in her arms. When she discovered my true nature, it was a real blow to the fantasy life she had imagined." He sounded sad.

"I know what it feels like to disappoint your mother, believe me."

"You know what's great therapy for depression? Senseless violence." He didn't smile; this time just held my gaze and smirked.

His even tone delivering that last sentence was chilling. His outbursts of disturbing comments were like a form of Tourette syndrome, and the more comfortable he became, the more often they would manifest.

A glass hitting the floor brought us back from our trip to therapy land. My eyes went looking for Norhan, but he was still in the same spot, uninterested in the chaos swirling around him.

Raine's voice screeched like a banshee in pain. Her face was red with fury, and her fists were flying toward the girl with the bob haircut. It was impossible to understand what they were yelling at each other, but Mata Hari was not taking the beating lying down. Her nails missed Raine's face by an inch and then turned around and went right back into attack mode. Raine's first hit landed like a wrecking ball, but the other woman didn't fold, she took the blow and bounced right back.

The match lasted less than five minutes, but it seemed so much longer. Two big guys, who I assumed were security, separated the two women and walked with them in opposite directions. Raine struggled with the bouncer, giving him a run for his money, but she couldn't free herself. I knew that if she got her way, the other woman would be on her way to the emergency room.

We were asked to leave. I thought about explaining that I had just met these people, but I didn't bother.

"We are going to this party in Queens, want to come with us?" Roman was already walking toward the subway.

"I think I am going to pass. Enough excitement for one night," I said.

"You don't know what excitement looks like, Andres!" Roman turned around, grabbed my shoulders, and started walking with me. "Besides, you live in Queens. If you don't like it, you can go home, and you'll be right there."

There was something forceful in Roman's voice. His tone was casual, but I knew it hid a threat. I was coming, like it or not. My heart started beating fast. His hand on my shoulder felt heavy, like a shackle attached to my skin.

CHAPTER 4

My face burned as if I stood in front of a roaring fire. I was tied to a vertical wooden pole. I was naked, my face staring at a brick wall and my back exposed to the unknown.

I tried to move my head, but a crown of barbed wire held me in place. Blood dripped from my temples and forehead in a thick, warm stream, leaving streak marks all over my face. The symbolism was no coincidence. Whoever put me there had a sick sense of humor.

Only my toes were touching the floor, but I could feel the sandpapery texture of the stone ground. The chill in the air pricked me like spikes on a mace. A dusky glow emanating from what I imagined were oil lamps turned the shadows of small objects into menacing figures. I was in a chamber designed for torments.

The scent of urine and feces overwhelmed my sense of smell. I gagged and felt a stream of bile rising in my throat, making it all the way to my mouth. I choked on it for a minute until the need for air became stronger than the pain chiseling my forehead. I tilted my head to let the murky fluid drip onto my chest.

I recognized the coppery and salty flavor of blood floating in the air, coating every corner of the room and foretelling my future. I knew my stenches were about to join those of many other people who had ended up in this place.

Death was dancing around me, taking its time, playing with my sanity before dragging me to the other side.

As if it were a distant thunder, I heard the whistling of the lash before it hit me. The leather strip ripped my skin apart, and blood started pouring from my back in a violent, gushing stream. My wails rose to the heavens like an imploring prayer, but there was nobody to hear it. The second, third, and fourth whiplashes landed full of hatred.

The fury and the speed of the hits increased as my screams became louder. My thoughts descended into a swamp of numbness and confusion, where the same question kept coming back like a stubborn child.

"Why me?"

I knew there was no real logic to what was happening. I was there because I had said yes to a group of strangers; it could have been any other fool.

I had not prayed for a long time. Even during my worst days, I kept God out of my business. I resented the all-loving and all-powerful creator for the cruel joke he had played on me. He'd made me weak in a family of fighters. I couldn't forgive him for that. But as the next strike ripped another piece of my body, I begged him to intervene, to make it stop.

I tried to remember the prayers my mother had taught me. *Dear Father.* Another brutal lash landed, and my brain scrambled to remember the rest. *Dios te salve Maria.* Another lash and the words stopped coming.

I saw the faces of the saints sitting on the fireplace mantel of my childhood home, and even though I couldn't remember their names, I implored them for their mercy. But God, as he always did, looked the other way.

"Please," I muttered when I was able to gather enough strength to say a word.

My pleas were answered with stronger punishment. I felt the wounds on my back extending like the roots of a growing tree. Agony replaced all my thoughts. The cold air touching my exposed flesh added to the hurt.

Urine flowed down my legs and onto the floor, blending with the burgundy pool growing at my feet. I had lost so much blood I knew it was just a matter of time until I bled to death. Sobs shook my entire frame, and even though the torment was unbearable, I didn't want to die.

"Please, don't kill me," I whispered.

An eerie silence followed my supplication. I heard the sound of heavy boots touching the floor, approaching without rush, making every step a source of fear and anxiety.

"You are a coward. I've had little girls who showed more strength and dignity than you." Even though I couldn't see his face, I could tell Ash was smiling.

"Please," I repeated.

"But I don't think you have learned anything, Andres. You keep talking. You keep demanding that I stop. You are an entitled servant. What makes you think you can take away my right to kill you? My property doesn't have privileges. You need to learn that." His voice sounded distant even though he was speaking right into my ear.

His finger stabbed one of my wounds, pushing into my body like he was reaching for my spine. I screamed, drunk in pain and unable to control my vocal chords. Ash kept talking, saying words I couldn't comprehend and digging into my flesh with the determination of a rabid mole.

My mind was trying to shut down, but the waves of excruciating agony wouldn't allow it. Ash grabbed my hair and pulled me back as far as he could without ripping my head from my shoulders. I felt the crown of spikes drilling into my skull, reaching for what was left of my deteriorating brain.

"I want you to thank me for the pain I'm giving you. I want you to understand that any second I dedicate to your worthless self is a gift." I could hear his words, but I had lost my capacity to comprehend their meaning.

I read somewhere that victims of torture could develop the ability to let their minds abandon their bodies and go to a happier place—a ray of rationality told me I had to try. I thought about Sunday mornings. I pictured a warm blanket embracing me like a loving hug while I watched cartoons in the living room. It was a sunny day, but the sun is dull during the winter in New England. My mother was trying to reason with Grandma Elisa, but she wouldn't hear it.

"Magali, *tu sabes yo tengo el gift*. Andres will need this," she said in a hushed voice that was too loud to count as a whisper.

"Elisa, I trust your visions," Mom said, exasperated, "but I think there are better ways to prepare the boy for when he lives in a place without heat."

"It is not any place, Magali," Grandma replied and crossed herself.

"You keep saying that, but you refuse to explain what you mean," my mother answered.

"Andres *no nos pertenece, mija*. One day he'll go back to the place where he belongs."

A splash of freezing water brought me back. My body started trembling, my jaw clenched with such force I thought my teeth would break into pieces.

"We haven't finished, Andres. There are still so many more fun things I want to show you. Don't pass out on me. It is rude, and you don't want to be rude to your master, right?"

"Why are you doing this?" I asked through my quivering teeth.

"Because I can. Roman told me you were an idiot, but I thought you would, at least, understand basic sentences. You are my slave. I can do whatever I want with you." His cheerfulness hurt.

Time became meaningless. Ash punished me for hours or maybe days; it was impossible to tell. Rounds of lashes were followed by his hands tearing my flesh. Every time I lost consciousness, icy water would bring me back, and the nightmare would start again.

The smell of burning skin woke me up. My throat was so shattered by hours of screaming that no sound came out of it even though I was fighting to release a loud cry. Ash was holding a hot piece of metal and carving what I assumed were his initials on my thighs.

"You are going to kill me," I whispered, half-unconscious.

"If you don't learn to keep your mouth shut, I will! You do understand that, right?" I didn't dare to answer. I just waited for the next hit to come.

I heard Ash pacing behind me. He was thinking of more creative ways to torture me.

"Maybe I need a different approach, a more humbling form of penance," his voice had a menacing tone.

The sound of his zipper opening wrecked the last crumbs of sanity in me. I heard the thundering clatter of a belt buckle hitting the stone floor.

"Ash, please! Please!" My cries were desperate. The hoarse voice coming out of me sounded insane and frantic.

He took his time. He was savoring this moment. Shattering my mind was as important as crippling my body, he needed to show me who was in control, I was nothing but another piece of his livestock, and he could do with me whatever he wanted.

His mouth was on my ear. His breath carried the flowery and putrid scent of a desecrated cemetery. He pressed his body against mine and clawed his long, hard nails into my hips until blood started dripping. He was breathing like an enraged wolf ready to attack, sweat dripping down his forehead and right onto my shoulders.

His skin felt rough and cold. He was about to rape me; that was the ultimate way to show me I was his property.

But he didn't. He just stood there, pulling me against him, knowing that every second that passed, fear and angst would drive me closer to madness. "In your dreams, slave. Maybe if you are good one day, I'll reward you with what you want so badly." He laughed, shoved me against the wooden pole, and walked away while pulling his pants up.

I started weeping until I blacked out.

**

I hit the floor with a loud crashing sound. Someone had removed the ropes holding me to the pole. I stayed there, moaning and aching, feeling my life energy dripping from my wounds and swirling down the drain at the center of the chamber.

I had no idea how much time had passed. In my exhausted mind, the session with Ash felt like both an eternity and a fraction of a second. The fact that it was over, that he was not there with me seemed strange. The word *slave* was imprinted on my consciousness. I was his property. He had the power to do whatever he wanted, enticed just by the pull of his will.

The cold stones calmed some of the pain in my chest. The relentless rubbing against the wooden pole had peeled a couple of layers of my skin, leaving a crust of blood on my sternum. I tried rolling over, thinking the icy floor could help the lingering agony in my back, but I didn't have the strength to do it.

My arms and legs felt like a colony of ants had moved into them. The tingling was weakening and constant, making it impossible to move them without the feeling that they would collapse and break. So I lay there, with my left cheek pressed against the ground and my gaze lost on the leather whip sitting right where Ash had dropped it.

I wondered if anybody was missing me already or if Josh had even noticed I was gone and called the police. It would be days until my cousin noted my absence. We shared an apartment, but our schedules almost never coincided. When the trash started piling in the kitchen and the toilet was covered by a black ring of mold, he would text me a *"WTF, the apartment is a mess!"* It would be many hours before he would become worried.

My family would think I committed suicide. My mom would beg the police to scavenge the entire city so they could recover my body, and after many weeks of doors shutting in her face, she would give up. My brothers would hate me for my selfishness, for putting Mom through the hell of my death, but even worse, for not leaving a body behind for her to mourn.

I knew I was the one to blame for my fate. I had let my starving neediness guide my actions and go against all common sense. I had opportunities to say no to Roman. I could have gone home after the fight at Tumultuous. I could have walked away when we arrived at that damn warehouse.

I don't know what I was expecting, but I lay there motionless, attempting to send my consciousness away. The faces of my family appeared in front of me like shapeless puffs of smoke struggling to condense into human features. I concentrated on the memories.

"The memories will take the pain away," I muttered.

I couldn't remember the address of our house in Bridgeport.

"It started with an eleven. Was it eleven fifty-seven or eleven thirty-seven? What was the street? I need to remember. How will I go back if I don't know the address?" But the details of my life stood at the edge of my brain like a word on the tip of my tongue.

I heard movement, soft steps like the sound of mice on a hardwood floor. It wasn't my torturer. Someone much lighter and more nimble was moving around me, picking up objects and dragging heavy things. The familiar sound of a mop let me know he was cleaning my blood, maybe preparing the scene for another round.

I closed my eyes and sobbed. The idea of more assaults to my body got me shaking. I was already a ragged mass of dislocated bones and torn skin; I was holding on to life by the strength of my fear. I knew that it wouldn't take much for my heart to stop beating.

A stream of warm water washed over me. The liquid felt like a healing ointment covering my wounds, and the pain started retreating like serpents slithering to their nest. I didn't know where it was coming from, but I didn't want it to stop. I let the drops of the curative potion shower me, and I felt life returning to my limbs.

The experience was like nothing I had felt before. My skin was growing back; I couldn't see it, but I could feel the cells reproducing at an accelerated speed and reaching out to each other, fighting to close the fissures crossing my back. The liquid kept pouring until it healed me. What would have taken weeks in a hospital bed had been achieved in minutes.

I couldn't and I didn't try to understand what was happening; it wasn't important right then. What mattered was that I was not going to die, at least not right away.

I opened my eyes and saw a pair of shoes splashed with bits of blood—my blood. I look upward into the pupils of a young man with brown eyes. He looked at me like I was a wounded animal.

He placed next to me a plain blue shirt, blue pants, and shoes.

"Get dressed," he said.

I was afraid of moving, fearful of the pain coming back, so I stood there motionless, paralyzed and frightened.

"You won't feel any pain," he said, as if he were reading my mind. "Get dressed, please."

I tested every muscle before launching into full movement. He was telling the truth. I was exhausted, but the aching was gone.

The garments he gave me were for a man twice my size. The material looked like cotton, but it was rough and stiff, and it radiated a whiff of ammonia and soap. He gave me a piece of leather rope and instructed me to use it to hold my pants up. His demeanor was matter-of-fact. He had no interest in knowing my name or any other information about me. He was there to complete a task, and he was determined to do it as fast as possible.

"What happens now?" I asked.

"You follow me."

"Can I ask where I am?" I took a chance because I knew he was a slave, just as I was.

"You are in Master Ash's castle. That is all you need to know."

"Where is this castle, in which city?" I asked.

"Please stop talking. It seems like after all that punishment you didn't learn anything."

We stepped into a wide hallway. There were no windows, but hundreds of chandeliers hung from the high ceiling, shining from within as if little suns were trapped in transparent prisons. It took a couple of moments for my eyes to adjust, but when they did it became clear we were not inside any building you would find in New York—maybe not even a building you would find anyplace in the twenty-first century.

The stone floors were uneven and brittle like the streets of Old San Juan. Curtains the color of the deep oceans bordered with silver velvet trim covered every wall. Yellow bricks peeked through the curtains, reminding me that I was trapped and giving the place a claustrophobic feel.

We kept walking a straight line, ignoring the smaller routes intersecting us along the way. I heard the voices of women laughing, the banging of pots and pans, the heavy steps of an army of people. The place was a hive full of worker bees concentrating on their tasks.

Every so often the drapery was interrupted by clusters of paintings depicting the same woman performing different activities. I couldn't help but stop in front of one of the canvasses. The picture was small but so powerful. Her gray hair was floating in the air while she ran through a snowy meadow, holding what looked to be the bloody head of a man. Her expression showed pride and exhaustion. Hordes of people and other creatures were witnessing her triumph and cheering her, Ash and his wife among them.

"Who is she?"

"Queen Ulda," he replied, "the ruler of this world."

I looked at him, puzzled.

"Get moving, this is not the Met." The reference surprised me. We were both strangers in this world.

"So we are both slaves," I said, fishing for solidarity.

"I'm nothing like you, and please stop talking."

Our procession ended in a square chamber with bare walls. There was no furniture, just three heavy and imposing metal doors standing in front of us like pathways to another dimension. There was a coat of arms at each entrance with the initials A. C. These were the same letters Ash had carved on me. The emblem had a spiky white flower in the middle, protected by two creatures with sharp, curved, saber-shaped fangs. But they were not tigers. The monsters looked like giant wolves with big ears pointing to the sky and jaws large enough to support their mortal daggers. Their coats were thick and black as a nightmare and their eyes envy green. The contrast between the delicate bloom and the ferocious creatures was perplexing, like everything else I had seen in that place.

"Stay here." My guide to this new world started walking toward one of the doors.

"Please tell me your name," I said with a tone of desperation in my voice.

I don't know why I did it; I just needed a gleam of normality. I thought the simple action of another human telling me his name would help me keep my sanity. It would help me remember that I had a name too, and I was not going to lose it.

"Carlos." His expression finally softened. "Your life from now on will be an ongoing nightmare. Be obedient, be smart, and you may survive." He walked away without another word.

I stood alone for a long time. Even though the idea seemed ludicrous, I searched the ceiling and walls, looking for cameras; maybe someone was watching me; this could be a test to see if I had learned my lesson. There were no real or mechanical eyes observing me, though. I was on my own.

I didn't dare to move, because the idea of escaping was ridiculous. I didn't know where I was, how big the place was, or where the exit was. Even if I found a way out, what was waiting for me outside? What I knew was that if I got caught, I would experience a slow and painful death at Ash's hands.

Two of the scarred giants I had seen at the party walked into the room. Up close I noticed their features were a lot less human than I had thought. The dim lights in the club hid their facial appearances. However, under the bright lights of the chandelier, their green reptilian eyes became obvious. Their faces reminded me of a copperhead snake. They had no eyebrows or eyelashes, only scales covering every inch of their faces.

Their presence was even more imposing than I had imagined. They towered more than two feet over me, and their frames were wide and stern as battle tanks. They didn't need weapons to do their job. They were organic killing machines, designed to crush anything and anybody that got in their way.

Pointing with their chins, they ordered me to start walking. We went through one of the doors into a dark corridor illuminated by transparent orbs hanging from the ceiling. Inside the spheres, flames danced on a bed of red liquid, providing a dim light that allowed me to see just a couple of steps ahead. I realized these were the lights illuminating the chamber where I had been tortured.

The hair on my arms rose, stirred by the sudden chill coming from the wet floor and the walls. As we kept walking, the temperature dropped at least ten degrees. We were leaving the warm and bright comfort of the castle and heading to the dungeons.

My soul was shattered, my nerves crippled, and my body traumatized, but at that moment, I didn't feel frightened. I knew a journey of torments and struggle was ahead of me, but after what I had endured, I took the idea of surviving another day as an acceptable consolation prize.

Ash had plenty of opportunities to kill me, and he had decided not to. Even though his psychopathic personality was as unpredictable as the path of a tornado, I figured he would have not "taught me a lesson" if he didn't want me to survive.

A set of stairs appeared in front of me, and if it weren't for one of the guards, I might have stumbled all the way down.

"You walk down there, slave," said one of the guards with a perverse smile on his face. Then they both turned around and left.

The murmur of many voices rose from the room at the bottom—groans and sobs of sorrow emanating from the dark hole before me. This was my final destination.

PART TWO

THE TIME OF DEMONS

CHAPTER 5

It is hard to explain how depression feels. Some people say that a black hole grows in the middle of their chest and starts devouring everything that is good and worthwhile in their lives until there is nothing left but sorrow. For me, it felt more like being possessed by a tortured spirit. There was no incremental sadness rising from my feet to my head. It was an instant internal devastation that took over in one big explosion.

I remembered the instant it happened. I saw the giggling faces of my teammates and the disappointment in my coach's expression. I heard my sneakers hitting the floor in the hallway of my high school. That was when the alien force took over me.

"Death will set you free," the ghost whispered in my ears while I ran home full of embarrassment.

I felt that old spirit haunting me as soon as I made it to the bottom of the stairs. I watched the scene like it was a play. But I knew this wasn't a work of fiction; it was my new life.

A heavy aura of misery hung in the air with a stinging odor of filthy and sick bodies. I started walking toward the back of the room, where all the beds were leaning against the wall. There were probably two hundred narrow bunk beds in total.

The tips of my fingers felt like stalactites ready to drop and shatter into pieces. The thin layer of fabric covering me was no match for the arctic air trapped in the room. Winter walked in the slave quarters, unaware or uninterested in the vulnerability of its inhabitants.

My clothing had no pockets, so I just rubbed my hands together, hoping the friction would revive my dead fingertips, but the shivering was unavoidable.

Adults of all ages huddled in small circles, trying to share the heat of their bodies. They were rubbing their hands with fury, some of them jumping in unison as if they were performing a ceremonial dance. I moved through the groups of people like a ghost. Nobody acknowledged my presence or even glanced at me.

Others were just lying on their beds, too sick to get up or too disheartened to care about hypothermia. I noticed bruises and scrapes big enough to be seen through the layers of filth wrapping their bodies. This wasn't just a place of suffering. I got the impression that death feasted in that room quite often.

The eyes of the men and women scattered throughout the barracks were empty, as if their souls had been vacuumed, leaving behind just a shell of flesh.

That will be me soon enough, I thought and tried to control my desire to break into pieces.

I wondered what kind of work these slaves performed. They were different from Carlos, lower on the food chain. They looked too weak for hard labor and too dirty for house duties. Maybe our fate was to be sold or even worse. We were there just for the sadistic entertainment of our masters.

I spotted an empty bed and decided to take it. There were no blankets or sheets, just a mattress made out of some rigid raw wool. I thought that sleeping on the floor would be more comfortable, but at the same time, the material might at least provide some heat.

I promised myself I wouldn't cry, so I channeled all my strength into keeping my eyes dry. I sat on my bed and thought of Ash's initials carved in my leg. He had removed my humanity. I was no longer a man; I was property, a thing that my owner could keep, break, or dispose of at will.

I heard once that dignity was not something that could be given or taken. It is something that humans choose to have no matter their circumstances. Whoever said that had not seen what I was witnessing.

I didn't know if it was day or night, but I was exhausted. Even though the healing water had closed my wounds, my body was still wasted. I wanted to sleep, but I wasn't sure how safe it was to close my eyes.

A woman walked toward me with purposeful determination. She was thin, but there was strength in her eyes that the other slaves had lost. She was also intimidating. It wasn't just her beauty—hidden under the layers of malnourishment—it was her smile.

I didn't want to talk to anybody. I just wanted to be left alone. I lay down and faced the wall, hoping this would discourage her and make her turn away.

"Hi, welcome to The Mist resort. My name is Claudia. Can I offer you refreshment?" She was standing next to my bed.

She held a small wooden bowl. I couldn't see its contents, but I was certain I was not eating it.

"I am ok. Thanks for offering." I did my best to sound friendly.

"You need to drink this or your wounds will reopen and get infected." Her face was serious but compassionate.

I sat on the edge of the bed.

"What do you mean they will reopen?"

"I mean they will come back. Nobody knows how this works. We just do what we are told. See that well?" She pointed toward the entrance of the chamber. "You have to drink from it for the next three days, and then you'll be fine."

There was no way to know if she was telling the truth, but I had nothing to lose. I had already lost it all, so even if Claudia had some hidden agenda, it didn't matter. I took the bowl and drank from it. The water was warm and a little dense. It didn't have a flavor or smell; it was just an innocuous broth.

"Thank you." I meant it. She was the first person to show me some kindness in a while.

"No problem, now rest. Tomorrow you'll have to work."

So we were workers.

"Where am I, Claudia?"

"I don't know, nobody knows. But you are not in Kansas anymore, Dorothy, that much I can tell you. You are not in Oz either."

I was surprised by Claudia's ability to find humor despite her circumstances. There was a spark in her eyes that had not been killed by slavery.

"What is our job?" I asked.

"We work the fields. It is hard work, so rest," she answered.

"Why did you call this place The Mist?"

"That is what they call it. The guards, I mean. I don't know if that is the name of the castle, the region, or the world. But we are in The Mist."

She attempted to walk away. I don't know what got into me, but I grabbed her hand, preventing her from taking another step.

"Please stay a little longer."

She pulled away.

A tall man with broad, bony shoulders came out of nowhere.

"We have a rule not to harm each other, but I will make an exception if you bother her." His voice was threatening.

"I am fine, Steve," said Claudia. "He's just scared and wants some company."

Steve kept his hostile eyes on me like a dog ready to defend its owner. Claudia walked away but then stopped and turned around.

"What is your name?"

"Andres," I answered in a low voice.

"I dated a jerk called Andres a long time ago. I hope God sent you here to redeem the name. It's a nice name." I thought I heard a laugh.

Steve left behind her without saying a word. I had arrived five minutes ago, and I already had someone who hated my guts. It was hard to think of ways in which my life could get any worse.

I stared at the knotted wood of the bunk above mine. Nobody was sleeping there, and I was glad for that. A strange calm came over me. Maybe it was the liquid Claudia gave me, but all of a sudden I was ready to sleep.

So much had happened in such a short period that my brain was not ready to process it, so it was doing the next best thing: shutting down. I knew I had to get more information. I needed to know where I was and who my captors were. I was sure my survival in this place would depend on that.

**

The banging sound of metal hitting stones woke me. I kept my eyes closed and wondered what Josh was doing up this early in the morning. Then I remembered Josh wasn't there, and I wasn't sleeping on his couch anymore.

I sat up and watched in awe the scene taking place in front of me. A trough running from wall to wall stood at the center of the room. Around the metal structure, a swarm of humans was kneeling, sticking their bare hands into the wide opening and slobbering over a slimy green substance.

"Breakfast," I mumbled.

I felt a violent urge to vomit, but I couldn't afford to be grossed out. My body was weak and begging for some form of nourishment. My insides were twisting and turning in noisy and painful ways.

I walked toward the food faster than I wanted. As I approached the eating area, I noticed the strong smell of burned sugar lingering in the air. It was like standing at the grounds of a scorched IHOP. The smell was sticky and cloying to the point of nausea.

I noticed there were no open spaces around the rack. Bodies were pressed against each other without an inch to spare. Those eating kept their elbows tight against their ribs and moved only their forearms and hands to reach for the food.

I was set to squeeze myself in when Steve blocked my way.

"New ones don't eat the first day. You'll get food tomorrow." He was enjoying delivering this news.

"If I don't eat, I won't be able to work. I am starving and tired and—"

"New ones don't eat! Did they hit you on the head when they brought you here? Are you not hearing well?" His voice got louder.

I knew I could take Steve if I wanted to. At some point in his life, he had been a football player or a professional wrestler, but now he was all bones and little muscle. He was still a big guy, but I knew I could push him to the side if I tried hard enough.

Even though my stomach was growling and my head was spinning, I decided to walk away. Following the rules was a good starting point to secure my survival. Even if this wasn't a real rule and Steve was just trying to mess with me, I thought letting him win this battle could be beneficial for the two of us.

As I headed back to my bed, I couldn't stop thinking, *Am I being careful or just a coward?*

I tried to think of a time in which I had fought for something important, but nothing came to mind. My whole life, someone had shielded me from violence and confrontation. My brothers protected me from the dangers on the streets; my mother, with less success, protected me from my brothers. I was not walking away because it was the right thing to do or even because I was afraid of Steve. I was walking away because I didn't know how to fight my battles.

Maybe it was the hunger or maybe just the anger piling on top of the hopelessness I was feeling that stopped me in my tracks. I needed to eat, I wanted to eat, and Steve's jealous-boyfriend stunt was not going to stop me from doing it.

I turned around and noticed he was still staring at me. The hate shooting from his eyes didn't scare me, so I walked straight to him.

"I don't want your girlfriend, dude." My tone was friendly but firm. "Actually, the last thing in my mind right now is meeting a girl. I just want to eat, and I will."

He looked at me, stunned, and without any warning shoved me. I barely moved. As I suspected, he was weak. I shoved him back and waited for the punch I knew was coming. The rising vein in his forehead and his puffing chest were signs he was not backing down.

I was ready to take him on. I actually wanted to. Beating him sounded like the perfect way to release my frustration.

"Wait there, newbie!" Claudia's voice came from the other side of the room.

There was an undeniable determination in her steps. The night before, I had thought it was just the urgency of letting me know about the healing water, but this morning it was there again. Walking like she meant business was just part of her personality.

"The two of you back down," she ordered and then looked Steve straight in the eyes. "Steve, please."

"I just want to eat," I said like a child making up excuses for misbehaving.

She gave us both a pointed look. "In this world we have nothing but each other. If we don't play nice, nobody will. Believe me, nobody."

Steve moved away without saying a word. Despite her good intentions, Claudia had given me a free entrance into Steve's hall of hate.

"Thanks," I said, avoiding looking her in the eyes.

"Go and eat. It looks gross, but it tastes ok."

As she walked away, I wondered why she was helping me. It was hard to believe that even in the cruelest of prisons, there were selfless people willing to lend a hand without expecting anything in return. The truth was, though, I didn't know if she wanted something in return or not. There was always a chance of Claudia coming back to me later and reminding me of how she got me food when I was starving.

I squirmed my way to the trough and started eating. The texture was the worst part. The slime seemed to be alive when it hit my mouth, moving from one corner to the other as if it had its own mind. There was something fizzy in it, like small bubbles exploding on my tongue, soaking my palate with a burned flavor.

My hunger was so uncontrollable I blocked my body's natural reaction of disgust and continued eating. Claudia was right. The flavor was not that bad. The sugar injected into my system gave me an unexpected surge of energy. I felt awake.

I saw Claudia talking to an older woman. She was consoling her. The woman's hands were trembling, and her eyes were swollen from hours of crying. Her skin was so pallid it looked like all color had been drained from her features. The sadness hunching her frame was devastating.

She was holding something in her hands. It looked like a bloody piece of fabric she was squeezing and twisting as if expecting blood to start dripping from it.

Claudia was obviously a leader among the slaves. She was the shoulder they cried on and the voice of reason. She was also one of the few younger women in the group.

I walked up to her as the woman was leaving. She greeted me with a smile.

"Her son was killed yesterday. Few people are brought here with family members, and I don't know if they are lucky for having a loved one or unfortunate for having to see them suffer. Tough call, right?" Her tone was sad.

"How did he die?" I asked.

"He didn't die. He was killed." Her voice was firm. "He stuck up for his mother one too many times."

We both fell silent.

"Who are our captors?"

"Nobody is certain. Some believe this is hell, some believe it is just another dimension, like a nightmarish Narnia." She smiled.

"What do you believe?"

"I don't believe this is hell. There are many people here who were practically saints before the catchers got them. Unless all we'd learned about hell was wrong, most of the slaves are destined to go to heaven when they die."

A questioning frown formed on my face when I heard the word *catcher*. Was she talking about Roman and his friends?

"Who are the catchers?"

"The monsters that capture and bring slaves to The Mist. They look human, but trust me, they are not."

Roman, Raine, and Norhan were my catchers.

"Is Ash a catcher?" I asked.

"I don't think so. Catchers are barely above the guards in the caste system. Ash is the big boss. His wife, Embla, is the lady of the house. I've heard house slaves call them sorcerers. Some kind of witch, I guess. There are all sorts of creatures roaming the grounds of this castle." She was getting restless. Talking about this place was not her favorite activity.

"What do you mean *creatures*? Animals? Monsters?"

"Both. You ask too many questions, Andres. That's going to get you in trouble. Keep your mouth shut and you'll find out soon enough what everybody else knows, which is not a lot anyways." She walked away.

I heard Claudia loud and clear. For the moment I would keep my head down and worry just about surviving and living another day. I got the impression I would have plenty of time to get the answers I wanted.

The memory of Ash's punishment made me shake. I felt a tingling sensation where the slashes had cracked my flesh and a phantom burning on the side of my right leg. The idea of enduring such an experience again terrified me. If anything, it would keep me from acting stupid.

The chattering of the morning routine turned into soft murmurs. There was a sense of restlessness and angst. I even noticed some of the slaves looking at me with fear. I guessed our working hours would start soon, and by the expression on everybody's faces, the hard part of our day was about to begin.

A current of boiling anxiety was making my hands numb. I was having trouble breathing and felt like the walls were closing in on me. It had been an intense morning, but I had to calm down.

I once attended a meditation class that, at the time, I thought was useless. As expected, I was not able to clear my mind and let my problems go, so I found myself feeling even more stressed out by the fact that I couldn't relax. I remembered the voice of the teacher and attempting to follow her instructions.

I sat on my bed, closed my eyes, and slowed down my breathing. I thought of a white light and did my best to keep my worries away. My mind kept fighting, running away from the white box, but I kept dragging it back with a force of will I didn't know I had. My heart rate became calmer, and my hands stopped shaking. It was working.

The guards appeared at the bottom of the stairs, and a frigid silence filled the room. The slaves started gathering at the center of the chamber like mice led by an enchanting flute. I followed and made sure to stand in the middle of the crowd, looking down, hoping to be invisible.

Ten guards stood in front of us. They didn't carry weapons. There was no need for them. Even if all of us attacked them together, we couldn't overpower them.

The giants stood in silence, sizing up the crowd. I saw a finger pointing at me. For the first time, I noticed his nails, white and curved like venom-dripping fangs.

"You." His voice sounded guttural.

My legs turned into water. I felt a hand pushing my back, and when I turned around, I saw Claudia's grieving face.

I put one foot in front of the other and moved in a slow, straight line until I made it to the front of the group. My gaze was on the stone floor.

"Pick a slave." His words were charged with hate.

I looked at him with confusion. His fist surprised me and made my knees hit the floor with such force I thought they were broken.

"Pick the slave you'll replace," he yelled.

I lifted my eyes and tried to ask for an explanation, but before I could articulate a word, the back of his palm sent me sliding on the floor.

"Last chance. Pick who will die so you'll live, or I'll kill you!"

Then I understood. When a new slave was brought, an old one was sacrificed. That was their method of population control. A healthy human would replace a sick one so that productivity wouldn't slow down.

I couldn't sentence another person to death. As afraid as I was of dying, the idea of choosing the next victim was beyond what I was able to do. For a couple of hours, I had forgotten where I was. I had thought my main concern was working on an empty stomach without realizing that heartless cruelty was now part of my life.

I knew that choosing death was not choosing a quick ending to my life. They would take their time. Maybe Ash would even do the honors and finish me. As terrifying as that was, I couldn't kill another man.

"I can't," I said, the softly spoken words falling from my lips like drool.

"Kill him," he spat to the group of giants behind him. Two guards walked toward me, stomping their heavy boots on the stone floor. I closed my eyes and waited, a strange peacefulness filling my chest.

"Pick me, I am ready to go!" The clear words of the woman broke through the frigid silence.

I saw the mother who Claudia was consoling standing in front of the main guard. Without saying a word, he grabbed her by the neck and snapped it. Her body became limp. Shit and urine dripped down her legs. He threw the body at the feet of the other guards, who grabbed her like a leaking trash bag.

"Dispose of it."

I saw their backs walking toward the stairs. My entire body started convulsing with sobs. Two small hands grabbed my shoulders. Claudia whispered words I couldn't understand. My eyes were clouded with tears, and my ears were filled with a loud and constant ringing.

CHAPTER 6

The white meadows covered in flowers extended vastly like the Great Plains. Small trails undulated across the fields like the tributaries of rivers converging into a larger path dividing the land right in the middle. It looked like a snow-covered plantation. The kind of place where slaves would harvest crops.

Rows and rows of transparent flowers reflected the pale light pouring from the sun. If I didn't know that slaves were tortured and killed on these grounds, I would believe this vision inspired Felix Bernard's "Winter Wonderland."

There were no trees, mountains, or hills, just a flat landscape the color of ocean foam rolling like a never-ending carpet.

It was impossible not to feel moved by its extreme beauty. Even in those circumstances—deprived of my freedom and fearing for my life—I knew I was witnessing something amazing.

We were walking in a single line surrounded by our vigilant guards. As we crossed the smaller trails, we were divided into teams of three.

"Grab one of those and start picking flowers, only the flowers, leave the stems behind." Steve pointed at the baskets waiting at the beginning of each row.

The blossoms were made out of tiny spikes clustered in groups of four, forming a sphere the size of a chrysanthemum.

Light and colors seemed to dance around the petals like a thread of rainbows passing from knot to knot. Even though the plants were transparent, there were faint red tints on the stems.

I started cutting flowers with my bare hands. The shoots would break with a slight twist, but the buds were hard as granite, and the smallest contact with my skin would draw blood.

There were thousands of slaves dressed in their plain blue uniforms, picking flowers. The entire human race was represented. They were all proof that the work of the catchers extended through the farthest corners of the earth.

The snapping of the stems broke the calm silence of the grounds. The clicking noise would rise in unison in a repetitive harmony echoing in the distance like a sad song.

"What is the name of this plant?" I asked Steve, who was just a couple of feet away.

"They call it eilift." He moved his lips without looking at me.

A warmth emanated from the eilifts, creating a temperate dome above the fields. I guessed the flower was a source of energy, but to power what? I had not seen any machinery since my arrival.

"What does it do?" I asked Steve.

"It gives eternal life."

My brain struggled to understand his words. I looked at the bulb I was about to cut and tried to wrestle with the idea of immortality. I remembered Roman's stories. His vivid recounts of New York in the twenties and World War II. He had not learned those facts in history books. He had lived them.

We—human slaves—were harvesting the source of our captors' everlasting existence. I felt sick and angry.

We were suspended in time. The sphere illuminating our labor was not moving like the sun I knew. Hours passed, and my shadow was still in the same position, following my steps like a dark stalker while sweat covered my forehead.

I worked in a state of disbelief. I was no longer in my world, and that undeniable fact was crumbling my brain. I was surrounded by monsters and magic, holding the secret to eternal youth, something that hundreds, maybe thousands, of men had dedicated their lives to finding.

"What is this place, Steve?" I whispered.

He didn't answer, so I asked a little louder.

"Shut up!" His voice was soft but his tone harsh.

"Sorry, I am just trying to understand."

"You are going to get us in trouble. This is not high school. Stop whispering." He moved a couple of feet farther so my voice could not reach him.

I paused to take a break and look around. I tried to locate Claudia, but it was impossible to discern one slave from another while they were hunched down.

It was obvious then that my dungeon was one of many where slaves lived. There were probably dozens or hundreds more in the castle. The place was the size of a city. Even if anybody dared to escape, finding the way out would be impossible.

"Where are they getting all these people?" I said to myself. "And how is it possible nobody misses us?"

Then I thought of Diana Gabaldon's prologue to *Outlander*. *"People disappear all the time . . . young girls run away from home. Young children stray from their parents and are never seen again. Housewives reach the end of their tether and take the grocery money and a taxi to the station."* All of them were around me. The young people, housewives, and kids from

Diana's imagination were all there working the fields of The Mist.

I didn't hear the guard approaching and didn't notice his hand on me until the sting of his fist in my stomach made me hit the ground. All the air in my lungs flew away.

He grabbed my hair with enough force to pull every single one from its root and forced my neck so far back that I thought it was going to break.

"Get back to work!" was all he said, and then he let me go with fury.

My face crashed the ground. The powdery substance covering the ground got into my mouth, flooding it with a nasty, sour taste. The fine white particles looked like Christmas Day snow, but they were something different.

I got up trembling. Tears were flowing from my eyes, but I wasn't crying because of the guard, it was something else. I felt a heavy sorrow landing on my shoulders, weighing me down with an unbearable feeling of hopelessness.

And then I wasn't there any longer. I was in my room, crying, staring at a pocket knife, knowing the blade would cut through my wrist at some point that afternoon.

"Andres, I am going to the nail salon. Are you ok?" My mom was knocking on my door. She knew something was up.

I took a deep breath and did my best to calm my shaky voice.

"Yup, Mom. Just listening to music."

She walked away without saying a word, thinking she was interrupting a "private moment." I grabbed the knife, and without allowing time to second-guess myself, I stabbed my wrist as deep as I thought possible. The pain made me light-headed, and I saw blood splatting in every direction. I pushed through the haziness, switched the knife to my other hand, and went deep into the other wrist. I screamed.

"Spit it!" Steve's firm voice brought me back to reality.

I looked at him, disconcerted.

"It's the snow, spit it! Clean your mouth!"

I spit over and over and scrubbed my tongue with the sleeve of my shirt until it hurt. The memories and the feelings started fading away with each stroke.

I sensed the eyes of the guard on me, so I grabbed my basket and continued working in silence. I was dizzy and disoriented. I looked at the scar on my wrist and wished I had that knife with me.

***

After a day of hard labor and nightmares, I lay down on my bed and let my body quiver with cold and hunger. The images from my past were gone, but I could still taste the horrible humiliation that led to my failed suicide attempt. It had happened so many years ago, but the feelings were fresh.

I was then an agonizingly shy sixteen-year-old, and the swim team was my only reason for attending school. In the water I felt confident. I felt normal. I was also a fool who thought a group of popular jocks would become my friends.

It happened on a cold Saturday morning at the beginning of spring. The night before, I had finally gathered the courage to tell Rebecca how I felt about her. After pouring my heart into that Facebook chat where we met every night, the most amazing words appeared on my screen: *"I love you too, Andres."*

I was then the happiest man alive. I told her so many sweet words. I shared with her poems I had written for her and diary entries dedicated to the feelings she sparked in me. I also told her that she had cured me, that at some point I thought I could be gay but she had changed all that.

I walked into that locker room with a smile tattooed on my face. I thought nothing could end my happiness. Life was finally bright. Then I saw the pictures posted all over the walls. Every single photo I had sent to Rebecca was printed and covered with mocking scribbles. My foolish love declarations were also printed for public display. The word *fag* was spray-painted on my locker.

I remembered my teammates laughing and repeating my words in scornful voices. Throwing in my face confessions I made to someone I thought was my soul mate, the one person who had ever understood what it was like to live in the shadow of someone and never measure up to the expectations of the rest.

She wasn't real. Rebecca was just the product of the twisted imagination of a group of teenagers bored to death and drawn to cruelty.

Dani found me that afternoon. He wanted to surprise the family with his visit, and instead, I surprised him by lying in a pool of blood. I always wondered why he even bothered calling 911. He wished I had died for what I'd done. He'd said it more than once.

I never told my family what happened in that locker room; neither did my coach. I just said I had been deceived by a girl I met online and the pain was too much for me to bear. Of course they believed me. Weakness was already my trademark.

The memories still hurt, and in the darkness of the dungeon, I cried. Soon my cries became loud sobs. Sick and dying slaves surrounded me; who would have cared that I was a coward.

"You have to keep it together, kid." Steve was standing next to my bunk.

I didn't care what he thought about me. It was already out of my control. I had been possessed by a spirit I knew well, and he was not returning my body until he had emptied it.

"If you don't stop, someone will come and make you stop. I am trying to help you." Steve was not the consoling type, but he was doing his best.

I didn't know what he meant by someone making me stop. Did he mean the guards? Other slaves? Somehow I knew I was not the first person to lose his mind in this place, and I doubted anybody cared enough to make me stop. Steve was lying as a way of calming me. In a weird way, it was sweet of him.

I was surprised by the warm and soft feeling of Claudia's hands holding mine. I looked at her through my watery eyes and saw a smile. Her brown eyes showed understanding and not pity.

"I know right now you wish you were dead. We've all been there. But the sooner you move on and embrace your new reality, the easier it will be to survive." She kept rubbing my hand. "You can lay there and let your body tremble, starve, and deteriorate, hoping that death will snatch you sooner rather than later, but when the time comes, you will run away from it, because we all do. So why put yourself through the pain of walking to the edge of life when we both know you won't jump?"

"I'm sorry."

"For what? For being human? For being afraid? Andres, nobody expects you to be a hero. Don't apologize for acting like a normal person. I just need you to calm down. We may not have hope, but we are trying to keep our sanity, and not letting misery take us over is part of that."

My chest stopped convulsing, and my jaw became still. I took several deep breaths and cleaned my eyes with the back of my hand. I felt like a little kid coming out of a temper tantrum.

"I can't say it will get better with time, that would be lying. But you'll get used to your new life. That I can promise you," Claudia said in a reassuring way.

I nodded. She patted my hands, got up, and said goodnight.

In the coming days, I kept my eyes down and my step brisk. I lined up between Claudia and Steve in the morning so that I would be assigned in the same area and then worked like a full-charged automaton until the guards ordered us to get back in line.

Even though my eyes were always in the flowers and my hands wouldn't stop pruning, even when blood was dripping from them, the threat of punishment was lingering and frightening like a bad omen. The monsters' steps echoed through the meadow like tanks on a battlefield, and just like the mechanical killing machines, they would trample innocents without looking back.

We lived in terror, and we thanked the deities we worshiped every time we survived a work shift unharmed.

Back in the slaves' dungeon, I did my best to learn how to survive. Claudia and Steve kept me close and taught me the basics. Steve was still not my biggest fan. He resented every second Claudia spent with me. I guess we were frenemies, and that was better than straight-out nemeses.

"Why us?" I asked them one evening after our shift. "Why go through all the trouble of traveling to another dimension to kidnap slaves?"

"Who knows," answered Claudia. "Maybe for the same reasons Americans got their slaves from Africa. They think humans are inferior, not worthy of freedom or dignity."

"Don't hold your breath for a Thirteenth Amendment, though," Steve chimed in. "You can see the hate they feel for us in their eyes. There is more to this story than we know. We, our species, did something horrible enough to them to start this whole thing."

"Why do you think we started it, Steve?"

"Because we always do."

All the information we had in the slaves' dungeon was nothing but speculation. Slaves didn't get history lessons, and even those who had been around longer had nothing but half-truths and questionable stories from their brief encounters with house slaves.

The source of most of the information and cautionary tales was Malcolm. He was an elderly slave with watery blue eyes and a serious craving for attention. Still, people respected him and trusted his knowledge.

"Take Malcolm's gossip with a grain of salt, but know that there is truth in it," Claudia lectured me. "He likes to feel important and has a tendency to exaggerate, but he is the only one with a legitimate friend among the house slaves. He knows things we don't."

Discretely, Claudia would point at different people and tell me what I needed to know.

"Don't mess with Margaret. She is sweet, don't get me wrong, but don't get in her business," Claudia said one night as we walked in circles the entire perimeter of our dungeon.

I grew to love those moments alone with her. I knew that it wasn't romantic. It was just a way to educate me without others listening to our conversation, but for me it felt as if we were taking a stroll around Central Park. Those walks were the only sliver of happiness in my miserable existence.

I took her advice as if I were a wizard's apprentice learning the ancient words to tame the beasts roaming an enchanted forest.

Steve's approach was less nurturing than Claudia's but as effective. "We don't hurt each other. If we have issues, we agree on someone we trust and ask them to decide what's best. That decision is law, remember that," he told me one night after I saw two young men arguing over leftover goo.

There was something tribal in the way the slaves organized. People like Margaret and Malcolm were clear leaders of their small groups. There were also those who took care of domestic duties and those who were there to protect the group. Tens of small tribes, surviving in peace despite hunger, pain, and sickness. It was admirable and hard to believe.

"You and Claudia don't seem to belong to any of the slaves' groups," I said to Steve one freezing night while jumping in place to stay warm.

"She is the final word in this place. She doesn't belong to any group, and she belongs to all," he answered in a serious tone.

"What about you?"

"I'm here to protect her from harm."

I swallowed too much saliva and choked for a couple of seconds. "Then what about me?" I said, worried about the idea of her life depending on my shaky hands. "I don't think I am proper bodyguard material."

"You are not here to protect anybody." Steve smirked and stopped jumping. "She wanted a pet." And with that, he walked away.

The next morning, I lined up ahead of Claudia. Steve's words were circling in my head like a dog chasing its tail. I knew he was messing with me, but my ego was still bruised. *I'm nobody's pet,* I thought.

We walked through the tunnels leading to the fields in silence. As the temperature rose, the air became thicker, charged with that incense smell I noticed at the party the night I lost my freedom. It seemed out of place, and I was positive it wasn't there the day before.

There was uneasiness in the air. The guards were tense and agitated. Their usual cruelty had been exacerbated by something we couldn't see. In a couple of hours, they yelled at and beat up so many people it seemed like they were trying to fill up a quota for the day.

As always, I worked without lifting my head and without stopping for more than the time it took to move from one blossom to the next.

The sun was scorching, and the air was thicker than the day before. That smell that reminded me of 7:00 a.m. Sunday Mass was everywhere.

The sound of heavy breathing grabbed my attention. I looked up and saw the young kid on my right standing motionless with his eyes wide open and his lungs wheezing like an old engine refusing to start.

"Hey, man, are you ok?" I said while going back to picking flowers.

The rhythm of his breathing got louder and shorter until total silence followed the hollow sound of his body hitting the floor. I knew it was stupid. I knew I would pay for my thoughtless decision, but I dropped my basket and ran to his side. The colors in his face were morphing into a pale shade of blue.

"Try to breathe," I said. His eyes were open, but he was not there.

I knew what I had to do. I had never performed mouth-to-mouth CPR, but I had watched enough movies to have a general idea. I pinched his nose, put my mouth on his, and tried to inject life into his lungs. I inhaled and did it again until I noticed he was breathing.

The guards were coming. I could hear their steps rushing through the trail. I didn't need to look at them to know their fists were aching to taste our faces.

"You need to get up, pick up the basket quickly." He wasn't getting any air, and his body was going limp; I knew my attempt to get him standing was useless. "Just try, they are coming."

The guard lifted me by the shirt and threw me to the side.

"Work!" he barked at me with a tone that, I guessed, was his version of mercy. He was giving me a second chance to leave without punishment.

I hurried to my basket and prayed for the kid to get up, but I knew he wouldn't.

The first kick lifted him off the floor and made him land several feet away. The second kick came with the unmistakable sounds of bones breaking. His face was a mask of pain and shock. His skin started turning purple again.

"You are going to kill him! Please stop!" I put my basket on the floor and started screaming.

The sound of the guy's ribs snapping and his skin splitting muted my pleas.

"A dead slave is of no use, the guy is sick, please stop!" I yelled, unable to let my brain take over the situation.

I was signing my death sentence, and I didn't know why I was doing it. Was this my attempt to commit suicide? Or did I care about the survival of a man I didn't know and who was destined to die sooner rather than later?

I felt Claudia's eyes on me. She was begging me to stay out of it. I knew what she was thinking: "He is already dead, and it is not worth it." But I was frantic, something had broken inside me, and a flood of frustration and rage was running out of my mouth.

"Leave him alone, you fucking monsters!" and that was what it took to make them stop.

They looked surprised and amused. I watched them walking toward me in slow motion, taking their time to let me know my death was approaching. I covered my face with my forearms and let them fall on me like a landslide.

I fell on the ground and stared at the dead eyes of the kid. His mouth was open. His skin was blue. I was sacrificing my life for a corpse.

Nobody came to my rescue. The snapping of the eilifts was the background music to my beating. The rest of the slaves knew better than to get involved in the punishment of a fool.

Blood poured out of my mouth, and I felt my bones on the brink of giving up; it was just a matter of time until I fell unconscious.

"Stop!" Ash's voice sounded like God speaking from the heavens.

Things were about to get worse. If the guards were capable of cruelty and senseless violence, Ash was the master of it. I remembered my session with him—the pleasure he took in mangling my body and my mind at the same time.

"I am surprised. Out of all these useless animals, you are the one standing up for someone." He was next to me, and his voice sounded pleased.

I didn't dare lift my eyes. I stared at the white powder inches from my mouth and begged he wouldn't make me eat it.

"Get up!"

Every movement was a struggle, but against all logic, I didn't have any broken bones.

"You." He pointed at Claudia, and my heart sank.

I didn't know what to do. If I spoke, the punishment would be worse for the two of us. If we survived this, I was going to lose the only friend I had.

"Grab him and follow me." Ash pointed at the raggedy body of the dead kid.

We dragged his corpse through several dark hallways. Claudia kept walking, with her back straight and her face blank. She was looking ahead right past me, making sure to avoid my eyes.

We entered a room that looked like a torture chamber. There were wood and metal artifacts with blades and chains hanging from them. Bloodstains and rotten flesh covered tables big enough to hold human beings.

My eyes burned with tears of disgust while I fought the gagging noises coming out of my throat.

"It takes some time to get used to it," said Ash, watching me choke with revulsion. "I like it. It reminds me of my place in the food chain."

He pointed at a table and told us to place the body there. That was when I heard the growls. A guttural sound, feral like the snarling of a wolf, emerged from one of the walls.

"Their hungry roars are like music. So powerful, so full of bloodthirst. The fenrir embodies everything that is great about our kingdom. Their brutality, their unapologetic will to take what they want." He was lost in his words. I could tell he wished he were one of those beasts.

I didn't need to see the monsters to know what they were. I had seen drawings of them when I was escorted to the slave quarters. Those things I thought were mythological creatures were demanding to be fed right under my feet.

"Cut the body into pieces and give it to the fenrirs. Detach the bones from the flesh—they prefer them separately—and then cut them into smaller pieces," Ash said with a grin on his lips. "I will soon send a guard to get you, so don't slack."

We looked at him with wide eyes and trembling lips. There was nothing to say. We had to desecrate the body of a kid who had just been beaten to death. That was our punishment.

"I hope you remember this act of mercy, Andres. I don't show my soft side too often, but today you impressed me. Just know that if you impress me again, I will kill you," Ash said. Then he walked out without another word.

Claudia was about to cry. Even the strongest of us has a limit. What we had to do was not only barbaric but scarring. Ash knew this. He knew that a wounded body heals a lot faster than a wounded mind.

"I'm sorry," I said, speaking for the first time in what felt an eternity.

"You were a hero—a complete idiot, but a hero. We don't get much of that around here," Claudia said.

I was surprised by her words. "I can do this on my own. You don't have to—"

"We are in this together," she interrupted, and started walking toward a rack stacked with all sorts of cutting tools.

"You cut the body in pieces. I'll remove the flesh." Her words were matter-of-fact, but I knew her soul was dying the same way mine was.

I pushed the serrated tool through the kid's body and noticed it was harder than I expected. As soon as I hit a hard surface, I started sawing with all my strength. The grinding sound of the bones would haunt me forever.

It took us hours to finish dismembering the body. We could have cut his limbs and bones faster, but without saying it, we agreed to do it with respect. We were not butchering meat. We were performing a mortuary ritual to say good-bye to a young man robbed of his freedom and his life.

The growls of the fenrirs grew louder as we delayed our task. We knew their fangs were dripping with saliva as their predator brains absorbed the smell of meat. Their eager pacing became stomping and their howls demanding. I ignored the chill on my spine, warning me that the monsters were tired of waiting.

The beasts' lair was connected to the butchering room by a wide opening in the left wall. There was no railing, just a cliff that didn't seem deep enough to keep us safe. From the edge, a cave the size of a cathedral extended deep and far, giving the place the appearance of a portal to a different dimension.

They were here first, I thought.

The cave's mouth exhaled a venomous smell. Its breath carried the weight of thousands of corpses that had rolled down those rocks and landed in the claws of the monstrous pack.

"I want to do it," said Claudia when it was time to throw the kid's body to the beasts.

"Let's do it together," I answered.

I didn't know why she was proposing such a thing, but there was no reason for her to go through the experience alone. Out of all the struggles we had endured that day, the final task was by far the most bruising.

"I want to do it. I am the closest thing he had to a friend or a relative, and it is my duty to return his remains to the earth."

There was so much pain and determination in her eyes. I wouldn't dare to question her decision.

As she prepared to feed the kid's remains to the beasts, I couldn't help but think about his soul. I was taught that innocents always go to heaven, but in a place like The Mist, in a place that seemed beyond the reach of God, where would his soul travel?

"Do you think he'll rest in peace?" I asked Claudia and then regretted putting the thought in her head.

"He will," she said and wiped her bloodstained hands on her uniform. "We are not in hell or in purgatory, Andres. We are not dead, we are still alive, and our souls are not trapped in this place. I refuse to believe that."

"I know, I feel the same way," I answered in a low voice.

Since my arrival I had believed that The Mist was just a world humanity had yet to discover. Maybe a parallel universe or a different dimension. Years of watching and reading sci-fi and fantasy had equipped me with enough knowledge to speculate for days.

"I know it is easy to believe that we are beyond the reach of God." Claudia was speaking to herself, I just happened to be there to witness her reflection. "But we are not. I refuse to believe that all this torture and cruelty is senseless. We are here because God wants us here. Because we have a mission to carry out."

I never thought of Claudia as the religious kind, and maybe she wasn't when she first entered The Mist. Like most humans had done for thousands of years, she was explaining her shitty reality through the will of an almighty who thought she was special enough to handle it.

I had a complicated relationship with the man upstairs, and if he had anything to do with me ending up in The Mist, I was sure it had nothing to do with a higher purpose.

"What was his name?" I asked, changing the subject.

"Leo. He was from San Francisco. He suffered from asthma. He was quiet but funny when he got talking." She was smiling, but her words were heavy with sorrow.

We put all the pieces into two wooden wheelbarrows and rolled them to the edge of the cavern. I took a step back, closed my eyes, and said words that were not prayers to any god, but good-byes and good wishes to a man I didn't know and for whom I had risked my life that morning.

Claudia threw the pieces one by one. The fenrirs caught Leo's body parts before they even hit the ground. Their fangs stabbed the flesh and crushed the bones with raw hunger.

After all was done, we sat in silence, contemplating the bloodstains on our nails and waiting for a guard to escort us back to our prison. Like a slideshow in my head, the images of coagulated blood gliding to the floor and human flesh piling next to us kept flashing in a macabre circle.

"Are you ok?"

She nodded. "I'll be fine." But I knew it wouldn't be that easy. I could tell that this was by far the worst punishment she had received.

***

By the time we were escorted back to the slave quarters, the chattering of the night was quieting down. People were getting in their beds, oblivious to the fate awaiting them in the far tunnels. We had decided not to share our experience. There was already enough suffering in this place without adding the fact that the afterlife started in the jaws of bloodthirsty monsters.

Claudia and I sat in silence, holding hands the way that victims of a near-death experience would. There was no romantic tone to it, just the need to know that someone else was there, that we were not crossing this daunting graveyard alone.

Steve stared at us. His facial muscles were hard like a granite sculpture. He was not ashamed of showing the jealousy boiling in his blood.

"Steve is in love with you," I said.

"This is no place for romance, he knows that." Claudia was warning me, the same way I assumed she had warned Steve before.

Under the layers of scratches and malnourishment, Claudia was still beautiful. Her eyes were big and brown like toasted almonds and her skin the color of that morning café cortado I missed so much. Her hair was a light-brown sea of curls, falling effortlessly over her shoulder. She was the astonishing result of a genetic symphony.

"Where are you from, Claudia?"

"Miami."

"I've never been there, but it was on my list of places to visit."

She stayed silent, staring at a horizon that was not there and scratching her hand as if she were trying to erase the history written on her palms.

"Do you have siblings?"

"It is getting late . . . We'd better sleep." She let my hand go and got up. I knew better than to try to stop her while Steve was watching, but I was not going to let her go either.

"My family is big, lots of cousins and uncles and aunts. Grandma Elisa is the only grandparent I have left. Her husband died many years ago, and my father's parents died when I was a teenager." I talked fast, hoping my words would hold her.

She interrupted me and looked at me, exasperated. "Andres, haven't we been through enough today? Do we need to talk about the people we love and we'll never see again?"

I knew her time as a slave had given her an armor that kept her emotionally numb. That night I was determined to break through that shell, so I insisted.

"I am the youngest one of three brothers. Their names are Dani and Jorge, and to be honest, I am not sure I would call them loved ones . . . it's complicated." I smiled and held her gaze.

She sighed and sat back down.

"You won't stop, will you?" she said with a defeated voice.

I took that as my cue.

"My mom comes from a big Puerto Rican family in Bridgeport, and my dad is from Tlaxcala, in Mexico. They are good people." I fought the tears rising up my eyes. "A little bit old-fashioned, but loving. My mom is quite overprotective, which may have messed me up a little."

She clasped her hands for a couple of seconds and then covered half of her face with one palm. "Andres, please stop."

"The morning before I was captured, I went to the pharmacy to drop off a prescription for Lamictal. Do you know what that is?"

"An antidepressant."

"Yup, a miracle in the form of a pill that was going to fix me." Her eyes softened. "Why were you depressed?"

"I don't know. I think I was born that way. Weak, emotional, a tad dramatic." I let the last word linger.

"You are not weak. You were the first person in here to try to help another man in years. That is heroic in this land." She put her right palm in my face and smiled. "You are needy as hell, though, and stubborn as a child in a toy store."

The heat flowing from her hand warmed my cold cheek. It took me a minute to recognize the feeling leaping from my brain to my heart: I was happy.

"I am an only child," she said. "My mom is black and my dad is Swedish. I lived in Stockholm for two years after college."

She cleared her throat and took a deep breath. She was looking for the words to tell a painful story, one I was sure she had not shared with many people.

"My mom has a huge family. They are very religious, but loving like you can't imagine. My dad is an orphan. He never met his parents, and he doesn't know if he has siblings. He grew up in a foster home." She dried her hands on her shirt and continued. "My dad moved to America when he was twenty and met my mom on his first day. I always thought that was romantic." She regretted that last word; her flushed cheeks gave her away.

"It is romantic," I said, dissipating the awkwardness between us.

"How did you end up here, Andres?"

"I followed this guy and his friends to a party that ended up being a trap. There were hundreds of people, I don't know if all of them were captured," I said.

"I was a junkie." Her words lacked any emotion. "I had not hit rock bottom yet, but I was getting close. My parents were fed up with me, and I was about to get evicted from my second apartment that year." Her eyes stayed on the floor. Her voice was low and full of shame.

I understood then why she was so reluctant to talk about her past. She was not proud of who she was, and I guessed she blamed herself for her fate. But so did I and, I guessed, so did many of the men and women surrounding us. That is the thing about victims of all kinds. They always blame themselves for the hurt they suffer.

Society was always asking us what we had done to deserve the misfortune coming our way: "Were you walking alone?" "What were you wearing?" "What did you do to make them hate you so much?" The perpetrators were never questioned. Their capacity for unlawful restraint and their evil nature were considered their free pass.

Victim blaming is the security blanket used by those who can't deal with the idea of evil or senseless cruelty. "That would never happen to me, because I'm smarter." "That would never happen to my daughter, because she is not asking for it." That is the only way some people can go through the dangerous journey that is life. Those who quickly jump to blame victims believe their good judgment and fake sense of moral superiority will keep them safe.

The sickest part is that many victims believe the accusers pointing their blaming fingers at them. That is why we don't speak up. That is why we tell our parents we tried to kill ourselves because a girl dumped us and not because a group of teenage boys played with our feelings and then humiliated us in front of an entire school.

But The Mist told a different story. Even though some of us had "asked for it," Claudia had told me that the majority of slaves were innocents. They had been captured and taken from their families at random, some of them in the middle of the night while sleeping safe within the walls of a home secured by an ADT system.

"Who captured you?" I was wondering if we were the prey of the same catchers.

"I don't know. I remember shooting up in my apartment, then waking up here. At first, I thought it was just a bad trip, that I would open my eyes and be back home, but when the withdrawals hit me, I knew it was real." She started picking at the wool in my bed and playing with it.

"I am sure that was hard."

"It was hell."

"But you survived," I said.

"Barely. Steve got me through it. He held my hand when I was trembling so hard I thought my bones would shatter and cleaned the floor when I threw up." She looked at him and smiled. "He doesn't hate you, he just doesn't trust you. He thinks you're a moron and that you'll get me killed."

"Well, that makes me feel better," I joked.

"He is a sweet guy. I have no doubt you'll become great friends."

"Thanks for sharing your story, Claudia."

I put my hand on her shoulder and thought about hugging her, but I knew she wouldn't like that.

"Don't get used to these moments of weakness, they don't happen often." She jumped off the bed and looked at me with soft eyes. "Have a good night, Andres." I stayed there. A warm current heated my body.

God, the universe, or whoever was in charge of existence had a sick sense of humor. I had to travel to a hellish dimension and become a slave to have my first real human connection. Madame de Pompadour, in one of my favorite *Doctor Who* episodes, said, "One may tolerate a world of demons for the sake of an angel." She was right.

The hard and itchy surface that was now my bed didn't feel as bad as it used to. My body was exhausted and my soul battered. Both were begging me to stop resisting and just go to sleep. As my consciousness faded away, I realized that something primal in the fabric of my being had been ripped apart. I was angry, and that anger felt like fire running through my veins.

After spending hours dismembering the body of an innocent just to feed it to a pack of animals, I decided that surviving was not enough. I was not going to spend the rest of my existence living as a slave. As insane as it sounded, I had to find a way out of The Mist. I was a Campos, after all. Heroism and strength ran through my veins, and even though I had never felt it, it was time to start digging deeper within my own soul. That night, as I was falling asleep, I decided I was going to escape, and I was bringing Claudia and, if he was nice enough, Steve with me.

***

A familiar scent woke me up. It was the middle of the night, and everyone in the slave quarters was still asleep. Soft snores and drowsy cries could be heard coming from different directions like the sad humming of a nearby beach. The exhausted bodies were recuperating from the aches of the day while their minds continued to live in a nightmare.

"This is the perfume of evil," I said, inhaling until my lungs were full.

I heard steps pacing up and down the perimeter of the beds. I lay on my side and opened my eyes just enough to see without seeming awake. I observed the lumbering figures looking at each slave, assessing them with inquisitive eyes. Their faces hovered over the sleepers the same way UFOs did in movies right before abducting a victim.

At first, I thought they were guards looking for someone to entertain themselves with. But these creatures were not as tall and massive, and their movements were too careful and silent.

One of them got close enough for me to get a clear view. In an instant my heart stopped beating, my lungs became paralyzed, and my mouth withheld a scream. The circles on his chest were unmistakable. I couldn't tell if it was the same one I had encountered before, but he was from the same tribe of the man who tried to kidnap me at the party.

I didn't dare move a muscle. I knew I had to close my eyes and pretend I was sleeping, but I couldn't. My eyelids stayed wide open, dazed like a child frightened in front of an audience.

I watched them inspect the beds, sizing up their potential prey with meticulous dedication. At some point, each of them stopped in front of a bunk and grabbed the hand of the occupant. They picked a man and a woman.

The two slaves had the blissful expressions of opium smokers and the same calmness to their movements. Their sight was fixated on a faraway point beyond the walls of their captivity.

They were walking away from my sight, so I repositioned myself to continue following their procession. The bed moaned as soon as I moved, and that was enough to make them look straight at me. Their heads tilted in an expression of recognition, synchronized as if they were a reflection of each other.

As they started approaching, I struggled to come up with a plan. The sheer idea of resisting a kidnapping made my pores ooze chilling drops of sweat. But after the events of the day, after witnessing a man die and then dismembering his body to feed ravenous monsters, I was done just letting fate mangle me like a lifeless toy.

They were almost next to me when a charge of heavy boots entered the dungeon. At least ten manic guards stampeded into the room, shouting orders. I saw terror in their faces, and the revelation stunned me. *The guards fear these creatures.*

One of the tattooed men gave me a pointed look and mumbled the word I had seen before on his lips: "Walker." This time, I had no doubt what he had said. Then they vanished. The four figures disappeared as if someone were erasing their existence one cell at a time.

"Everybody up!" the guards yelled.

They grabbed slaves furiously, dislocating bones as they threw them on the hard stones. Their violent outburst saw no mercy for the weak or the sick; their madness was uncontained.

Before I had time to react, one of the giants snatched me and threw me out of my bed. I got up without complaining and rushed to find Claudia, but in the middle of the chaos, it was impossible. I ended up next to Steve.

"What's going on?" I whispered.

"The hidden ones took two slaves." He sounded worried.

They were called the hidden ones, and they had visited before. The revelation intrigued me. But what was even more unexpected was the effect these creatures had on the guards. I suddenly understood Roman's fury at the party. Back then I had thought he was defending me, but he was in fact attacking an old enemy.

Why didn't he just disappear? I thought, remembering the brutal beating that hidden one had undergone.

"Two are missing." The guard's voice was stern and irritated.

The monster at the center of the room was without a doubt a higher rank. There were so many scars covering him that his skin looked like a cluster of veins fighting to escape the constriction of his body. The amber webs spreading through his face were only interrupted by his reptilian eyes.

He took a woman by her neck and lifted her without effort. Her feet were pedaling in the air as if she were trying to escape tentacles holding her at the bottom of the sea. We all knew how this would end.

"Where are they?"

The woman didn't have an answer, and the guard knew it. Even if she knew what had happened, his hand was squashing her vocal cords so hard there was no way she could speak. Her face was red, and her eyes looked like they were about to pop out of her skull.

He was just taking his frustration out on her. We didn't know where the missing people were, but I was certain we all knew who had taken them. The guards would not have entered the room stomping like an invading army if they didn't know who they were facing.

They are afraid, I thought, and a surge of excitement shook my core.

The guards were not invincible killing machines. They had a weakness after all. I had no idea if the tattooed men were better or worse than our captors, but they knew how to frighten them, and that was what we needed.

The woman's body was going limp. Her legs were keeping up the fight, but it was just a matter of seconds until air, and her life, abandoned her body.

"I saw the men who took them!" My voice echoed in the chamber like a bell and surprised not only the others but myself.

The guard let go of the woman out of sheer astonishment. His eyes were staring me to submission, demanding to know how I dared to speak.

"They had blue tattoos all over their chests. There were two of them." I kept my head up.

The room got silent. They were all preparing to witness my death. I bet most of them thought I was asking for it . . . for the second time in twenty-four hours.

"They have a smell . . . the men with tattoos. It is like a mist, it sticks in the air, and you can taste it," I stuttered. My confidence was draining as the giant approached me. His march was threatening like a shotgun and, I knew, just as deadly. I clenched my jaw and made probably the most stupid decision I had made so far. I was going to challenge him.

"Where are they!" he yelled.

"They left. They are not here. Why do you keep asking us? How would a group of slaves know what these creatures are or where they go?"

The back of his hand hit me. I fell to the ground like a log, and he kicked me in the ribs like he was trying to bring down a wall.

"How dare you speak to me that way, you filthy animal! How did they escape?" he yelled while kicking me one more time.

When his foot gave me a break, I managed to say it. "They disappeared into thin air."

He looked confused. His primitive mind tried to comprehend what I was saying.

"He is telling the truth," Claudia yelled from the crowd.

Steve was right; I was going to get her killed. But then the rest of the slaves followed her lead. Anonymous voices clamored. "The creatures can appear and disappear at will!" Everybody had seen it.

The crowd got rowdy, and while shouting unintelligible insults at the guards, one by one, men and women surrounded me, creating a human barrier. The stunned hulks stood there motionless. Their eyes jumped from one slave to another as if they were witnessing a dam about to burst and had no idea how to contain it.

I took the opportunity to get up. Steve grabbed me and let me lean on his shoulder. They had broken a couple of my bones, no doubt.

"Thank you," I said in a voice that sounded closer to a moan.

"You are an idiot," he said.

I was both scared and proud. Witnessing this catharsis gave me hope and made me feel human again. But I knew that acts of rebellion cost lives.

"Shut up!" the boss screamed.

But the floodgates had opened, and the slaves kept shouting. The energy in the room started rising, and the tension built. From the middle of the crowd, Margaret's voice rose.

"'We shall overcome, we shall overcome, we shall overcome someday. Oh, deep in my heart, I do believe, we shall overcome someday!'" she sang.

Timid voices joined her until the song was loud and clear like the notes of a clarinet.

The guards knew that there were two options: start crushing skulls or let the slaves win this battle.

They looked at each other and, without saying a word, just walked away. I knew we would pay for this the next morning.

When Claudia walked up to me, I was still holding on to Steve, the pain in my chest rising. It was becoming harder to concentrate on anything else.

"I'll get you some healing water, you'll be fine," she said, sounding worried.

"Who are the hidden ones?"

Claudia shrugged "We don't know. For a while I thought they were a myth—they don't come here often, and they don't always take people with them."

The chorus of slaves was still chanting. Tears were rolling down their faces, and some of them were hugging each other in heartfelt embraces. Their spirits were not crushed and dead as I thought in the beginning. There was still fight in them. Just like me, they wanted freedom, and just like me, they had no idea how to find it.

Steve and I started walking toward the well. Every step generated a current of pain from my chest to the top of my head.

"The guards fear those creatures," I said.

"The guards don't fear anybody, they are just annoyed by them," Steve said, irritated.

But he was wrong. That morning we had smelled the tattooed men in the corridors leading to the fields, and the guards were on edge. While we didn't know why then, now it made sense. The guards knew their enemies were close.

"I saw it on their faces, Steve, trust me. They fear the hidden ones."

"Even if that is true, it doesn't matter to us." Steve stopped walking and looked into my eyes. "You know my job is to protect her. If you keep putting her at risk, I will forget we are friends, Andres," he threatened.

"I don't do it on purpose, Steve."

"But you keep doing it. On purpose or not, if she suffers because of you, I will make you pay."

"You mean that in the friendliest way possible, right?" I said, mustering sarcasm I didn't know I possessed.

"I'm warning you. That is as friendly as I get."

I nodded. I realized that by Steve's standards, we were close.

Several days went by, and we had not seen or smelled the hidden ones. Since their last visit, the guards had increased their brutality, and even though nobody had died, their constant punishments were enough to crush our spirits.

Slaves were chosen at random and tortured for hours. We were forced to watch and listen to the screams of men and women who were already too sick and too tired to endure such cruelty. Our captors were making us pay with blood for our small act of rebellion.

I spent all my free time thinking about the men with the blue tattoos. I relived the scene at the party over and over trying to uncover details I may have missed, but I didn't find any clues or connections to our captors. He had called me walker; that had to mean something.

"What's in your head, *mijo*?" Lidia sat next to me and patted my leg.

She was the mother figure among the Latino slaves. She was also the official translator and one of the favorite referees when conflict arose.

"Nothing, just thinking."

She reminded me so much of my mother that every time we talked, I felt like crying.

"Thinking is considered an extreme sport around here. Don't think too much; all the thinkers end up dead."

I thought of sharing my questions about the hidden ones, but I wasn't sure what to say. Should I tell her one of them had given me a nickname? Or that I thought the guards feared them? I opted for keeping my conjectures to myself.

"Don't worry, Lidia, I'm not plotting a revolution," I said and laughed.

"That's what Fidel told me . . . I didn't believe him either," she said, winking at me.

"Do you believe we could one day fight for our freedom?"

"After what happened the other night . . . maybe. But this place is not only about organizing and fighting. We are facing forces no human has faced before." She kissed my forehead and got up. "Don't get crazy ideas in your head, *mijo.*"

CHAPTER 7

A new slave was brought into the quarters several weeks after the incident with the guards. He was received with the same indifference I felt on my first day, and his face had the identical expression of pain and confusion I was wearing the evening of my arrival.

He stood at the bottom of the stairs, taking it all in, observing the scene with the clinical concentration of someone who has learned to assess every place before taking a first step. His chest was rising and sinking fast. His eyes were red and watery but had not lost their anger and frustration. I knew the feeling.

As I got closer, holding a cup of healing water, I recognized him. The memory came back like a flashback in a movie. It was Lakay, the homeless kid I had met in the subway.

Roman and his friends were still hunting in New York, and now they were targeting kids. Nothing was off-limits for them. As long as they were strong and healthy enough, even the most vulnerable were fair game.

"You need to drink this for the next three days or your wounds will reopen."

There was surprise and recognition in his expression. No doubt I had made an impression with our first interaction. I was certain it wasn't a positive one.

He grabbed the cup and drank without asking for further explanation. "You are the perv from the subway." His words were flat and hurtful.

"I'm sorry about that. I didn't mean to come across creepy. I was just trying to—"

"Whatever, dude, I have met plenty of guys like you. I don't need to hear your bullshit," he said and rushed away from me.

I knew not to follow him or try to explain myself. The fact that he had encountered depraved jerks in the past was not surprising, and the fact that our first encounter had set off his alarm was not shocking either.

"You know the kid?" Claudia asked.

"Kind of. We had a weird exchange in the subway the night I was captured. He thinks I am a perv."

She looked at me warily. "What did you do to him?"

"I offered him twenty dollars. My heart was in the right place."

"To do what?"

"Nothing!" I said, offended. "I just wanted him to get a good meal, but I didn't say that, so . . ."

Her head swung from left to right.

"So you scared him."

I nodded.

The next morning, Lakay didn't even attempt to eat. He stayed on his bed, playing with his clothes and mumbling to himself. Every so often he would move his arms and finger as if he were playing an invisible harp.

He was strong for his age, no doubt. I imagined that his current bed was no worse than the places where he crashed every night. He didn't come across as a kid who would go to the shelter.

The air in the room was heavy that day. The elderly and those who were sick walked around with a sobering demeanor. We all knew the kid held someone's life in his hands.

New arrivals were not warned of this tradition by order of our captors. If the guards suspected the slave knew what their first duty was beforehand, they would make them pick two sacrifices instead of one. It had happened many times, and on several occasions, the guards' suspicions were wrong.

The giants with the cracked skin entered the room as expected, and Lakay was called to the front. He kept his head high, but against all his will, the subtle tremble in his chin was visible. His hands were clenched tightly behind his back, and his knees were locked and unyielding, preventing his body from collapsing.

It was déjà vu. He was asked to choose a slave, he looked confused, and a back slap sent him crashing onto the floor. But he realized what was happening a lot faster than I did. Just one hit, and his face showed understanding. He nodded, tasted the blood on his lip, and looked straight at me. The guard walked toward him, and Lakay lifted his palm. He had made a decision.

Claudia looked at me in terror. Her eyes were wide like a scared deer, and her mouth hung half-open, trying but failing to whisper something across the room. I moved my lips so she could read them.

"Don't worry."

Lakay's eyes were full of hate, but I knew it wasn't directed at me. It was against what he thought I represented, against all those men he had met before and thought were part of my tribe. He didn't want to punish me. He wanted to get revenge on them. I was the offering, the sacrifice that would mitigate his anger and his hurt.

I felt sorry for him. Even though he was ready to cut my life short with the power of one finger, a flood of sadness and clarity washed over me. I was in front of a boy so angry and so damaged he was willing to sentence a complete stranger to death based on one conversation. The troubles and insecurities I had carried for so many years seemed so insignificant compared to his suffering.

"It is fine," I muttered, looking at him.

I was ok with dying that morning. The more time I spent in The Mist, the more I felt like there was a higher power orchestrating my expedition through hell. The sudden appearance of Lakay was just another sign. Maybe the last sign in my journey.

I closed my eyes and waited for the words to thunder.

"Him." Lakay's voice was faltering.

I heard the guard's steps, and I prepared for the air to be squeezed out of me. Claudia was the only face in my mind. My family had lost me already. They wouldn't mourn my second death, but she would.

I opened my eyes when I heard the drowning scream of an older man. The sewer-like smell of his dripping, lifeless body coated our nostrils, and it was over. He was being dragged upstairs. He was now breakfast for the fenrirs.

We were taken to the fields right away. As soon as I was assigned to my row, I picked up my basket and started cutting flowers with a heavy weight on my shoulders. A man was dead, and the soul of a boy had been corrupted, but we still had to work like any other day. We didn't have the right to mourn the dead. We were farm animals kept alive by the grace of our master. The real misery of being a slave was not physical punishment, the constant hunger, or the hard work. It was the slow but steady crippling of our souls.

It is amazing how the body becomes accustomed to hard conditions. We learned to live with a void in our stomachs.

We got used to existing in a constant state of exhaustion. We endured pain and broken bones and then just walked to the healing well and got ourselves ready for another round. But there was no healing for the spiritual bruises. Watching others die without dignity never became easy; seeing their bodies treated like roadkill was always disheartening; looking at the guards' grins of satisfaction was always enraging.

The petals went right through one of the bloody crusts on my fingertips. The red drops falling to the ground released the pressure building in my veins. I felt the tectonic plates of my feelings rearranging and getting ready to release the seismic energy building in my ribcage.

Concentrate on the pain. Pain will erase everything else, I thought while letting another prick touch my finger.

There was something growing in me, a polluted substance multiplying and taking over my cellular structure. I could see the helixes in my DNA turning putrid green. The Mist had killed my spirit, and now it was rotting inside me.

My past struggles seemed so stupid compared to what I was living. I looked at my former self from the vantage point of my new reality and felt embarrassed by that boy screaming for attention with a blade in his hands.

"Everybody's feelings are valid," my therapist had said many times, but she was wrong.

Her advice had done nothing but justify the poor decisions I made in my life. She convinced me I had the right to feel sorry for myself, that my depression was not a sign of weakness but an emblem I should wave like a flag in the faces of those who dared to criticize me.

Someone should tell people like me our feelings are bullshit, and we should just snap out of it, I thought.

I couldn't change my past, but I could learn from it. I saw the pale ground tainted with amber dots dripping from my

fingers and realized the key to my spiritual freedom was staring me in the eyes.

I grabbed a handful of white dust and put it in my mouth. I
heard a warning scream as reality started fading. But it was too
late. My consciousness was already standing in the dungeon
where Ash had tortured me for the first time.

The lashes felt as real as that day. The blood dripping into
my eyes stung even harder, but then it was washed by the tears
that wouldn't stop flowing. Ash's footsteps got closer, and then
his finger was digging the raw flesh in my back. I knew what
was coming. I was about to black out.

I heard myself crying and begging, but my feelings were
not the same. The guy screaming was someone who used to
occupy my body, the idiot who had given Ash what he'd wanted
that day. I knew that the monster was feeding on my suffering.
Every squeal was ambrosia for his psychopathic mind, and I
was a free, all-you-can-eat buffet.

*I can't change this, but I can take the power away from
the memory. I can make it a source of strength and not fear,* I
thought.

There was a lucidity in my thoughts I didn't feel the first
time I tasted the snow. I was in control—the pain was there,
the angst was there, but the fear was disappearing.

It was when the shadows of pain were about to swallow me
whole that I heard it.

"You can't kill him." It wasn't Ash speaking. The voice was
unmistakable; it was Roman. He was there that day. He had
witnessed Ash's artistic work.

"I can do whatever I please, Roman." Ash's voice was full of
exasperation.

"Balthazar tried to save him at the party, and he called him
'walker.'"

"The walker is a myth, Roman. And even if he was the walker, what better than killing him right now?"

"You know the prophecies as well as I do, Ash. What if he is the worlds walker? What if we can break him and find a way to take his power away?"

"I still believe killing him would be better," said Ash, disappointed.

My shoulders started shaking while two hands held my mouth open. I was back in the field. Claudia and Steve were on top of me.

"Have you lost your mind?" Steve yelled. As soon as my eyes were open, he walked away.

Claudia's hands were still inside my mouth. I pushed her fingers away and sat up.

"I am fine. I am fine."

"You are clearly not fine," she said furiously.

The guards seemed confused by what was happening. They moved in my direction, but after a couple of steps, they changed their minds. I grabbed my basket and went back to work, expecting a punishment that didn't arrive.

I couldn't stop thinking about Roman's words. He thought I had something he could use. He thought I possessed a certain power he wanted to take from me. That was the only reason I was still alive.

As enticing as the idea of being special was, the most important piece of this new knowledge was that now I knew my captors would think twice before killing me. That was a big advantage in this world.

***

The next day, Claudia was not talking to me. She lined up away from me so we wouldn't be assigned the same area. I didn't blame her. I had caused her enough trouble already, and it was better if she kept her distance. My recklessness could bring her nothing but pain or even death.

I worked the way I did during my first weeks. I kept to myself; I moved fast and followed orders. Still I felt the eyes of the guards tracking my every step. I was on their radar, they didn't trust me, and their instincts were spot-on. Behind my silent and submissive labor, a pyre of revolutionary ideas was brewing.

The shift ended, and I was unharmed. I counted myself lucky.

Back in our prison, I approached Margaret.

"You have a beautiful singing voice," I said.

"What do you want, boy?"

"I want you to sing more, I want you to gather people and sing songs that talk about hope and freedom."

She frowned, skeptical. "Are you trying to get me killed?"

"I just want to make our lives more bearable. We need to regain hope. This"—my finger made a circle pointing at the dungeon—"cannot be the end."

Margaret shook her head and walked away. The next night, a group of black slaves led by Margaret were singing songs written during the civil rights movement. The pride and smiles on their faces was enough to warm the entire place.

A couple of evenings later, Lidia grabbed my arm as soon as the guards left after a day of hard labor.

"Let's go for a walk, Andres." Her grip was firm.

"Everything ok?"

"I don't know," she answered.

We walked the confined space of the quarters in a circle as if we were taking a stroll around the park. The hairs on my arms were standing, maybe because of the chilly air that danced around the dungeon, or because I knew I was in trouble.

"Many years ago, there was a young man," she started saying. "He was handsome and strong, like a wild dark horse. He was also sweet with women and caring with those in need."

"Your husband?" I asked.

"My son, Carlos." Her voice was heavy with pain.

I wondered if he was the same Carlos who had greeted me after Ash was done with me.

"What happened to him?"

"He decided to speak up, to defend the sick and the elderly." She took a deep breath before continuing. "He stopped being afraid."

"So they killed him?"

"The master's dog—the catcher with the sulfur eyes and the tight clothes—took him away." Lidia was talking about Roman. "There are fates worse than death, and I'm sure the dog knows many of them."

She stopped walking and faced me. Her eyes landed on mine with the heaviness of a death sentence. "You remind me of Carlos . . . in the best and the worst ways." We continued walking.

"I take that as a huge compliment."

"It is, but just like my Carlos, this world is changing you in a way that it doesn't change many others. It is making you braver, bolder, and reckless—"

"Is that a bad thing? Becoming braver, having hope?"

"I don't know, Andres. In my experience it is. The Mist has awakened something long dormant inside of you, and I'm worried."

"Roman thinks I have something he wants," I said, and felt embarrassed by the implication of being somehow important.

"Did he tell you?"

"He said it to Ash to stop him from killing me."

She frowned and bit her lower lip as if she was trying to find the best way to share a hard truth. "Just be careful, Andres." Her sweet smile ended the conversation, and she wished me good-bye.

Lidia was right. Every day that went by, the anger inside me became harder to handle. The guards' cruelty fueled my hate and frustration. The feelings boiling inside me were an engine running wild.

***

Claudia got over her anger and started talking to me again. I was thankful for her friendship, but I knew I couldn't get too close. I was a time bomb, and she was the last person I wanted to hurt if suddenly I went off. I hung out with her and Steve in the dungeon, but during the working day, I made sure to stay at a safe distance.

A couple of weeks into this routine, she started noticing that every time she lined up behind me, I would find an excuse to move to a different spot. At last she demanded Steve and I tell her what was going on.

"Steve didn't tell me to stay away from you, Claudia," I said for the second time. "I promise."

"I told him not to get you into trouble," Steve added.

I gave him a look that said, *You are not helping, dude.*

"So the two of you have conversations about me and make decisions regarding what's best for me?" Claudia's voice was angry. "Do you think I am a child?"

"Claudia, nobody is making decisions—" I started explaining.

"When you decided that it was safer for me if you stay away, you did make a decision for me!"

"He is a little unstable, Claudia. You have to admit it," Steve interjected, continuing to be unhelpful.

Her eyes threw daggers at him.

"Claudia, I am going through some stuff," I said, my mouth dried out. "Trust me. It is best if I keep my distance when the guards are close."

"I think I will keep my distance from the two of you for a while," she responded. "Or at least, until you learn that I'm not some trophy you need to protect or fight for."

She left Steve and me staring at each other, not knowing what to say or do.

CHAPTER 8

Embla and her friends walked into the field around midday. They were intoxicated. Their steps were unsure, and their laughs persistent and loud. They were stumbling through the rows of slaves like they had just learned how to walk and equilibrium was still a huge accomplishment.

"All this is mine!" the lady of the house said, lifting her arm with a gesture she thought made her look royal.

The two other women giggled while following Embla's gaze. The three of them were dressed for the crowning of a queen. Their long and exuberant gowns sparkled with intricate embroideries covering almost every inch of the fabric.

Embla looked nothing like the mangled doll I had seen the first time. Her neck extended like an ivory Tuscan column adorned by the sculpture that was her face. She reminded me of the Venus de Milo: tall, beautiful, and damaged.

Her friends were less-flashy versions of herself. They could have been her sisters or just members of the same clan. The resemblance was obvious, though, and when they laughed together, they sounded like the same voice sung in three different octaves.

They were looking to entertain themselves by tormenting us. Like vultures scavenging for carrion, the three women circled from one slave to another, smelling their fear and assessing their weaknesses. When they found the perfect victim, they would attack them with slaps, insults, and sexual advances. Then they would cackle away to their next target.

Nobody was safe—men, women, old, and young were left behind shaken and embarrassed. The more they flinched, the more Embla and her friends enjoyed it. They fed on the slaves' humiliation. They gorged on the feeling of superiority.

I kept my eyes down and continued working like everybody else. Their squawking increased and decreased in volume as they moved from one side of the field to the other.

I raised my head when I heard them next to me. Their faces had the distorted grimace of those whose happiness depends on poison. Their breaths carried the thick scent of moldering fruit mixed with sweet and earthy tobacco.

Embla grabbed my face with her right hand, forcing my lips into a pout. "Dirty slave want Mommy to kiss him, right?"

The other two exploded in laughter.

My eyes were right in front of hers, but I kept my gaze down. I knew they would move on soon. I just had to let them have a little fun and then get back to work.

"You are the especial one," she said to herself, "the one Roman likes."

Embla slid her free hand under my shirt and felt my chest. "I get it . . . not bad . . . and people say we don't feed you well here," she yelled, turning around and looking at her friends.

Her hand kept gliding down my torso, stopping at the place where the rope held up my pants. Her fingers ventured a couple of inches below my belt.

"Is this awakening anything, boy?" She gave me a drunken wink.

"It's not, ma'am," I answered, still not looking her in the eyes.

"You smell like the fenrirs' lair!" She pushed me back and walked away.

I stood watching them as their clumsy stroll continued.

Just a couple of minutes later, I recognized a soft gasp. Claudia's neck was pushed all the way to her right, and her chin was facing the sun, her expression begging to escape the grasp of the three women. I couldn't hear what they were saying, but I could see their hands going under her shirt and into her pants.

The energy of an eruption rose from my core, violent and thoughtless. The world around me vanished, and all I could see was her panic.

"They'll kill her if you go there," said Steve.

"They're raping her." I was fighting the knot of ire and tears in my throat.

"They will stop soon, the same way they did with you."

But I couldn't wait, I had to take their attention away from Claudia and back to me. He was right, if I went there, they would kill her, but if I made them come back to me, they would kill me.

"Ladies, if you want to have fun, I have all the fun you need right here!" I yelled while grabbing my crotch in a way I never thought I would.

The women looked at me like three confused pigeons. Their heads tilted and their eyes wide while I continued to yell obscenities. I didn't look at Claudia; I was embarrassed by what I was doing and couldn't dare to see the same embarrassment reflected in her face. But it was working. The three harpies let her go and started slithering toward me.

"I promise you that I'll make it worth it!" I yelled.

Embla's face turned purple, her jaw clenched, and her hands turned into fists. The silliness of her earlier expression was gone.

"Come on, lady! You said you liked what you touched," I yelled.

Her hand pointed to the sky, and in an instant, a group of guards put their brusque hands on my arms and dragged me out of the field.

We entered the great hallway in a section I had not seen before. Men and women dressed in clean slave outfits were rushing from one door to another, carrying all sorts of shiny dishes, bowls, and trays. None of them gave me a second look. I knew from my interaction with Carlos that to the house slaves, the field workers were a lesser breed.

I noticed steam and spicy aromas coming out of the rooms we were passing. We were still in the service area, probably the kitchens of the castle.

"Since you are in the mood for fun, I think you will love to attend our party," Embla said, mocking me.

I was going to be entertainment or maybe even a meal. I knew so little about the world of The Mist that the idea of cannibalism fit within the margins of reality.

We stopped at the first fork we encountered in the hallway. Embla looked at the guards with a tight smile on her face.

"Get him ready," she said and then walked in the opposite direction.

My hands were drenched in sweat. I knew there was a severe punishment coming my way. I had asked for it. I didn't regret my actions, though. I had done what was right to protect Claudia. If I survived, she would yell at me for jumping to her defense. I could almost hear her voice: "I have survived on my own for a long time, Andres. I don't need your help. I don't want the burden of your death on my shoulders." Of course she was correct. I had no right to play hero.

"Where are you taking me?"

The walking snake looked at me in disbelief. "To the showers," he said and shoved me for no reason.

The bright and vast hallway started shrinking and becoming darker as we walked. We arrived at a wide opening where a dozen men and women were standing naked under running water while a group of house slaves scrubbed them with anger and disdain.

I saw Carlos working on a woman with legs so red and so bony they looked like long fingers with prominent knuckles. He glanced at me for a second and then went back to cleaning her.

A female slave approached us and stood in front of the guards, waiting for instructions.

"He will not be used by the guests," the giant informed her and then left.

She was as short and solid as a construction worker. The creases around her eyes showed at least forty winters in a land where heat depended on your ability to cut a tree. She wore her hair up in a tight bun.

"Take your clothes off"—she pointed at my ragged uniform—"and follow me."

"What did he mean by *not used*?"

"They won't rape you," she responded without an ounce of emotion in her voice.

"That is why you are washing the other slaves?"

"We don't do chatty around here. Please be quiet."

She motioned for me to stand under a pipe from which water was pouring. I took my place and shivered as the freezing stream hit my skin. The woman grabbed a brush so big it seemed designed for horses and started scrubbing me as if she were trying to erase me from existence.

I contemplated the disheartening scene taking place around me. Humans treating other humans like animals. It wasn't something new. I had seen such acts in my own world, but there, in a place where we were all under the thumb of supernatural monsters, it seemed even more saddening.

"How can you do it?" I asked her.

She looked at me, surprised and annoyed.

"Better them than me," she answered sharply.

"So house slaves betray their own kind in exchange for what? A more comfortable bed? Better food? Less torture, maybe?"

"You have a big mouth and very little understanding," she snapped back.

"Then enlighten me. What makes it worth it to prepare men and women to be raped and tortured?"

Without warning, she grabbed my balls and started squeezing. The pain made my knees weak.

"Not being raped and tortured, that is what makes it worth it." She squeezed a little tighter. "Don't you dare judge me. You have no idea how long I've been in this place and what I've gone through." She let me go and went back to furiously scrubbing me.

The woman worked on me for a long time, and when my skin was burning, she walked away without saying another word.

The guards came back a couple of minutes later to escort me to my final stop. I walked naked and cold, my skin red and burning with embarrassment. We reached the banquet room in no time. I was welcomed by a chorus of laughter rumbling in the room, rolling like a wave from one end to another. The guards tied me to a wooden pole facing a window that comprised the entire wall. The eilift fields were shining in front of me, interrupted only by the silhouettes of the slaves who were still working.

"This piece of filth is looking for fun," Ash yelled to the adoring crowd. "I say we give it to him." Euphoric cheers broke out like the sound of a bloodthirsty jungle.

Roman walked in front of me and got his face inches away from mine. His eyes were glowing with flames of anger and frustration.

"Moron," was all he said and then he strolled away from my view.

Ash's slashes stroked me like lighting. His fury traveled through the bloodstained lash and exploded on my back in shards of pure hate. He wanted me dead, but he wanted me to take a slow and painful walk to my final breath. My lips stayed tied together, glued by a fury growing in me like terminal cancer.

PART THREE

THE BLOOD IN A HERO'S HEART

CHAPTER 9

The sweet liquid touched my mouth, but my lips didn't move. The creases where my defiant words rested were swollen and bruised. He beat me until my vocal cords were paralyzed by the proximity of certain death.

I couldn't open my eyes. Every inch of my skin was punctured by what felt like thousands of needles. I grunted. The surface scratching my back was making the stabbing insufferable. I wanted to move. I wished I could get away from the torturing place holding me hostage, but my limbs ignored my orders.

My memories came back in blurry and incoherent flashbacks. I stroked the walls surrounding my consciousness as hard as I could, but only slivers of recollections made it through the cracks. There were laughs and cheers. Ash's voice was vibrant, full of joy and commitment to the task.

"He killed me," I mumbled.

The dark and rough prison where I was lying had to be my grave, but slaves didn't get graves, they got fed to the sacred beasts of the kingdom.

"It is not working. I've never seen it not work." Her voice was distant and sweet, like the sound of a carousel inviting children to ride.

"Give it time. He is pretty mangled." There was concern in his tone. He was trying to calm her down, but he didn't believe his words.

"He is dying. Even this potion has its limits." Her voice was trembling, and for some reason, that made me happy. She cared if I died.

"Give the guy some credit. He is a lot stronger than you think."

I wasn't dead, there were people fighting to keep me alive, and they were losing.

"I wonder why Ash didn't kill him?" she asked.

"There are worse fates than dying; don't count him lucky yet," he answered. Someone had said that to me before. I couldn't remember who. She probably nodded. His statement was as true as the agony in my flesh.

Why didn't he kill me? I thought.

Ash said he would end me if I surprised him again, yet there I was, still breathing. Maybe Roman had stopped him. Perhaps he still thought I had something he wanted.

My awareness started declining. Their voices became unintelligible until they were just white noise. I was dying. *Even magic has its limits,* I thought. Then I was out.

***

My screams woke me up. I attempted to sit up, but the pain held me down like chains. I stared at the wood above my head. I couldn't remember where I was.

My entire body ached, but my face was the worst. I felt like a giant, uneven rock was sitting over my shoulders. My cheekbones bulged like hills in a black-and-blue valley. My lips had doubled their size. Punches had poured over my face after I passed out from the whipping. That was obvious.

The nightmare felt so real. Ash and Roman were torturing Claudia, and I stood paralyzed, witnessing from a corner. Every effort to rescue her crashed into a bolt of agony that jerked my entire body and make my knees land on the cold, rough floor. I tried to scream, but my voice sounded hoarse and breathless. She was crying, calling my name, and begging me to make them stop.

"You have to take it easy. For some reason, the healing water is working slower than usual. I think it has to do with how badly you were beaten." Steve was standing next to my bunk.

"How long have I been out?"

"Two days."

I ignored my bones and muscles and just pushed myself up. The current of hurt that rose from my feet shot from my throat as a loud moan.

"And the guards let me stay here while you guys were working?"

"It took some convincing. Two men almost died, and I had my share of punishment too, but they gave up in the end," he said as if those sacrifices were not a big deal.

Why were people risking their lives for me?

"Where is—"

"She is fine," he interrupted me. "Embla was so out of her mind by your performance she forgot about her."

Steve gave me another cup of water. I swallowed it with one gulp.

It was the middle of the night. Everybody else was sleeping. He had been keeping an eye on me.

"I'm worried about you, Andres, but I'm more worried about her."

"I was just trying to defend her," I replied.

"She didn't need defending. She has endured torture like that and worse before." He looked down and let the thin line of his lips relax. "I think this has a lot more to do with you than with her."

"I'm not sure what you are trying to say, Steve."

"You have changed. People are noticing, and people are impressed. I think you know that, and you like it." His words were an accusation.

"I'm not looking for attention, if that is what you think." The conversation was taking a tense turn.

"But you are getting it, and attention gets you killed around here. Attention can also kill those you love," he said while raising his voice.

"Thank you, Steve, I hear you."

"Andres, I am your friend. I may not be the kind of friend who tells you he loves you and hugs you when you are down, but I am a friend you can count on. She is my priority, but I want you to be safe too."

"I know," I said, and the tears I was holding back made my entire body ache. "I know, Steve, and I promise you I will try."

He nodded and walked back to his bed.

I had to work the next day. I couldn't let others risk their lives just to save mine. If the healing water had not done its magic by then, I would deal with the pain. Besides, part of me wanted to show Ash, Roman, and their troop of monsters that I wasn't defeated. If they were trying to teach me a lesson, they had failed. The punishment had done nothing but feed the fiery anger burning in me.

My eyelids got heavy and shut. I had so much to ponder, but my brain was still frail. I knew the future held nothing but more struggle. I had to figure out how I would walk that path without getting killed and without killing others.

The now-common sound of the morning woke me up. The aches in my muscles had subsided, but moving was still difficult. I sat up and let the still air in the dungeon fill my lungs. I wasn't hungry. The burned and sweet smell of breakfast made my stomach roll in discomfort.

Claudia rushed to my bed with that purposeful spring I loved.

"You look like crap," she said, smiling.

"I'll bet I do."

"Stay in bed another day; the guards are done fighting us on this."

"I want to go to the field," I said. Pain still accentuated my voice.

She shook her head and blew air through her nose. I knew she was counting to ten.

"What got into you?" she held back the reins of her annoyance.

"I don't know, or at least I'm not sure yet."

I attempted to get up; her hands hurried to catch me. "I am angry," I said, limping and straightening my back.

"We all are, Andres."

"You know that is not true, Claudia. Most people are hopeless, not angry."

Her expression was hard to read. I could see her brain connections sparking, trying to make sense of a guy who was crazy, stupid, or both.

"If you are working today, you need to eat something." She decided that changing the subject was the healthy thing to do.

I nodded. I had pissed her off enough already, and I wanted her to stand next to me during the day. Her presence would give me the strength I needed.

The eilift fields were always a vision. It was hard to believe that so much beauty could bloom in a place irrigated by nothing but suffering. I looked at the sky, and the glorious, immovable sun was still there, in the same place we had left it the day before.

My basket felt heavy even when it was empty. My arms trembled like the leaves of a dying tree. My feet struggled against gravity and dragged me forward one inch at a time.

I sensed Claudia's and Steve's looks of pity all through the morning, but I kept my head down and worked as if the throbbing in my body were not real. I knew I had the strength to get through my shift. It was just going to take a lot more willpower than usual.

"Hurry up!" The voice of the guard and the pressure of his palm against my back startled me.

I attempted to pick up the pace, but it was a daunting task. I locked my jaw and squinted as I pushed my legs to move faster. However, my efforts had little effect.

"I said hurry!" Another shove, and as I stumbled ahead, a burning sensation whipped my bones.

"Not feeling so brave today, Andres, right?" He knew my name. That was a dreadful omen.

He pushed me again, hard enough to make it hurt but soft enough so I wouldn't fall. It was a game for him.

"I'm sorry. I'll try to move faster," I said, realizing what he wanted.

I had to prove to him I had learned my lesson. He wanted me to show the other slaves I was defeated.

He thrust me once more, this time hard enough to make me fall. I screeched when I hit the ground. He chuckled and walked away. Nobody came to help me. Nobody said a word. I just gathered my mangled bones and went back to my duty.

By the evening, the potion had done its magic. My limbs regained their strength, and the indigo spots Ash left as a reminder of his power were fading to a light-blue color.

The properties of the healing water were a complete mystery to all of us. We drank it without questioning and enjoyed its health-giving gifts as if regrowing bones was as normal as growing hair.

At first, I thought that the well stood there as a symbol of mercy, proof that our masters had a thread of humanity in their souls. But I soon learned that their gift represented the complete opposite. Instant healing gave them the opportunity to punish us until life was just a whisper and then fix us and start all over again. Their magic was nothing but another torture device.

I was falling asleep with this thought rambling in my head when the perfume I had been waiting for surprised my nostrils. I heard footsteps approaching me, and before I had a chance to sit up, his hand was covering my mouth.

"Quiet," he whispered.

I recognized him, so I nodded. I was not about to lose the opportunity to learn who these creatures were and why the guards feared them.

His fingers wrapped around my hand without squeezing, and a gentle current overcame my body. The fatigue I had carried with me since my first day melted onto the floor as an involuntary smiled bloomed on my lips. The world became brighter, and I could feel its luminosity on my skin.

I got up slowly. The shapes in the room started bending and mixing until they all looked like a Van Gogh painting.

A rushing river of dark matter swallowed us and dragged us in its current until a splash of light brought us back into the world.

We were standing in a room buzzing with activity. Slaves in blue garments moved from corner to corner like members of a trading caravan carrying treasures from one shore to another. I could hear a roaring fire and smell the sweet aroma of Thanksgiving emanating from a table full of golden roasted birds. The incense smell of these creatures was mixed with the perfume of real food, making my mouth watery and eager.

The most striking part of the scene was the faces of the slaves. They looked happy and healthy. The smiles on their lips had erased the wrinkles left by their lives as slaves. They moved with a purpose, propelled by a sense of safety that didn't exist in the barracks I had just left behind.

"Where are we?" I asked.

"This is our church. Here is where we bring the slaves we can rescue."

My brain struggled to process his words. The creature who attempted to kidnap me was a religious leader.

"My name is Balthazar, and you, Andres, should eat," he added.

I walked behind him, taking in every detail. There were no chandeliers or lamps hanging from the ceiling. We were in a place where crystal stones shone as bright as the frozen sun in the fields.

The place had the proportions of a gothic cathedral. Tables, beds, and benches took up most of the space. There were close to five hundred people and about fifty tattooed men that I could see. All of them were engaged in tasks that ranged from cleaning dirty dishes to sword-fighting practice.

A chubby woman, like I hadn't seen in The Mist since my arrival, walked in front of me, carrying a pile of linens as tall as she.

"How do you do?" she said in an accent that reminded me of Mrs. Weasley from the Harry Potter movies.

The place had all the characteristics of a fairy-tale trap. It was a house made of candy, with shiny walls and a warm fire inviting children to feast until they were full and ready for the witch's oven.

He gave me a plate and pointed at the table in front of me. Vegetables, of colors I had never seen, covered the wooden surface. Towering birds stood majestically, waiting to be carved. I had seen *Pan's Labyrinth*. I was not about to touch anything.

I had so many questions and didn't know where to start. Balthazar stared into my eyes and tilted his head from side to side the way he'd done on our first encounter.

"You don't need to be afraid. We won't hurt you." His voice was soft and reassuring.

"You were not particularly friendly when we met," I said with more hostility than I intended.

"There was great urgency and no time to explain. I was trying to save your life."

"You could have said so," I snapped.

He looked at me the way parents look at their children when their small brains cannot grasp an idea. It was a mix of annoyance and tenderness.

"Andres, your face was drawn in ancient books. Prophecies have announced your rise for centuries. I recognized you as soon as I saw you, and I panicked. You were among the slaves. I had to get you out."

Roman was right, these creatures thought I was more than just a plain human. This was the part in every fantasy movie where the hero finally understood why he always felt different, and every odd event in his life at last made sense. But that wasn't my case. I never felt different. Snakes didn't speak to me in the zoo like they did with Harry Potter. I wasn't able to notice the homeless when nobody else did, like Richard Mayhew in *Neverwhere*. On the contrary, I always felt extremely ordinary, one of the many losers who walked through life knowing he was destined to mediocrity.

The idea of a deeper meaning to my suffering was enticing, even comforting. But I wasn't "the chosen one." Roman didn't kidnap me because fate said he should. He did it because I let him.

"You got the wrong guy, Balthazar. I have a really common face—"

"I did not get the wrong guy. But we can talk while you eat. I'm sure you are hungry." He gestured for me to sit.

I sat on the bench and studied his face. The same features that had caused me panic now seemed friendlier, even caring.

"Eat. What is the worst that can happen? Your life is a living hell already." A smile formed on his face. He was right, I had nothing to lose.

The meat melted in my mouth like a spoonful of savory and sweet cream. The rich texture of the vegetables glazed my taste buds with a spicy sensation. There were acidic and sour drops of flavor in the sauces, balanced with touches of salt and sugar. I didn't know how much my body missed real flavors until my plate was empty and my brain was overwhelmed by endorphins.

He sat next to me and started talking without waiting for my questions to pour over him. "We are called augurs. For millennia, my people guided the decisions of rulers, making sure that peace, prosperity, and kindness were the pillars of the kingdom." He patted his legs as he looked for the words to continue. "Our eyes can see the weaving threads of time. Images of the consequences of each decision manifest in front of us, warning us about the dangers ahead." He cut a piece of something that looked like a pie and put it on my plate, as casually as if we were two old friends catching up. "Since the beginning of time, our word was sacred, and our advice was considered divine," he stated with pride.

"What happened then?" I asked.

"Two thousand years ago, the first eilift grew in the fields." He paused, looked into the fireplace to his right, and took a deep breath full of anger and sadness. "At first, we didn't know what it was. But the augurs knew that its existence would bring our world into an era of darkness and cruelty. We warned the queen. We told her to destroy it. But she was overtaken by fury and grief. She saw the crystal flower as a trophy, a present from the gods who were proud of her actions."

I couldn't make any sense of this. He was retelling the story as if the missing pieces were things I should know.

"When did humans come into play? Why enslaving my kind?"

"Humans were the reason behind the queen's ire. It was a human who betrayed her and the blood of a human what birthed the first eilift. She thought it fitting for your race to take care of the fields."

"So we don't only harvest them. The blood dripping from our fingers every day makes the flowers grow," I said as if repeating the words out loud would help me make sense of the sick story I was hearing.

"You have to understand that the eilift not only gives eternal life. It also transforms those who consume it. It makes them cruel and violent."

"I guess, then, that augurs don't take it."

He smiled proudly. "We don't."

I let his words sink in. The monsters that had enslaved us were immortal, and we were working their fields so they could stay that way. Anger boiled in me like a geyser about to erupt. Thousands of humans were being tortured and killed just so the queen could take revenge on some guy who wronged her.

He placed his hand on my trembling fingers, and the storm of feelings dispersed. He had the power to manipulate the way my body felt.

"We share your anger and your pain," he said.

"Your people are not slaves. You aren't being tortured and killed so that demons can live forever."

"Many augurs have died in the name of this war. Torture and death are not strangers to us. This struggle is ours too, not just yours," he said firmly.

I entangled my fingers as if I were about to pray. My eyes were staring at the floor, holding back tears of frustration.

"Why are all these slaves still here? Aren't you bringing them home?" I asked. I thought the crowd seemed too comfortable to be preparing for a departure.

"We can't bring them home. Only catchers have the power to cross to your world."

"And none of them are helping you?" I asked.

"No, and they never will."

"So what is the plan? You keep bringing slaves here, giving them a better life until they die, and you have room for a new one?" I sounded angry.

"We are forming an army."

I couldn't believe what I was hearing. Did he want to train humans to start a war against hordes of monsters? The idea was ludicrous.

"You need fifty humans to take on one guard, and I have seen Roman kick your ass. If all catchers are like him, then they are as hard to kill as the giants."

If they had the ability to see the future, they should have known an army of men and women had no chance.

"No creature is invincible, Andres. Some are just harder to defeat than others."

"Why not just find a way out? Why not obligate a catcher to free the slaves? This is your war, not ours."

He was not being completely honest with me, I could feel it. I was open to believing the augurs were the good guys, but I also knew they had their own agenda.

Balthazar gave me a friendly smile. "You are becoming stronger. Your true nature is growing. Soon your intuition will become one of your greatest weapons."

"Answer my question," I said, not letting him change the subject. We were not talking about my imaginary superpowers, at least not yet.

"We need numbers," he confessed. "There are not enough augurs left to face their armies, and nobody else in The Mist will help us. Humans are our only hope."

I couldn't help but wonder if these slaves had a real idea of the high and bloody price of a revolution. Most people had only learned about uprisings and revolts through books. They had never heard the screams. They had never heard the tanks rolling through the streets. They didn't know that most revolutionaries die without seeing the change they fought for.

I looked around me. The men and women living in that church were there willingly. They knew what their role was, and they were more than ready to play it.

"So how do you kill an indestructible monster?" I asked.

"They can be cut," he said. "Not by just any weapon, a regular blade will never pierce their natural armor, but their skin can be penetrated."

"If a sword won't do the job, then what?"

"A blade forged from the bones of a willing hero."

The secret to our masters' demise was a weapon made of human bones. The Mist was not a kind place for my people, no matter what side of the war you were fighting on.

"So is your plan to skin some of these people and use their bones to arm your soldiers?" I said in a challenging tone.

He shook his head.

"No . . . we are not sure what such a weapon would look like, or even how to make it . . . the prophecies are not as detailed as we would like," he said.

"That is why you have not attacked yet. You need to figure out what this mythical bone weapon looks like," I said, sounding frustrated.

"That is part of it. But weapons are not all that we need. We also need you, Andres."

"Balthazar, even if my face was the face you saw in those prophecy books, you need to know I'm not the hero type."

"The sword that will end the age of darkness has to be wielded by the worlds walker—that's you."

"I don't even know how to answer to that," I replied. The more he talked, the more confusing and overwhelming the conversation became.

"I know it is a lot to process, Andres. But you have to believe me. The sooner you understand, the sooner we can end this nightmare for your people and mine."

Discovering that you are good at something, that you are special in any way, has two very distinctive sides. First, it makes you happy. It makes you feel important and even above others. But then comes the realization that now those around you have higher expectations. The revelation that you are more than just average brings the heaviness of responsibility and constant self-doubt.

"What exactly does the prophecy say about the worlds walker?"

"It tells the story of two brothers. Twin brothers born of a human woman and a creature of The Mist. One will be known as the worlds walker. The other will be known as the prince of worlds. Their hatred for each other will trigger the final battle. The victorious brother will lead The Mist into an age of compassion or sink it deeper into darkness."

I smiled and let out a sigh of relief. "I don't have a twin brother, Balthazar."

"Prophecies are not always literal, Andres."

I wondered if the humans living with the augurs thought I was the champion they were waiting for.

"Do they also believe I'm your worlds walker?" I asked, pointing at the slaves.

"They don't. They know we are waiting for a hero, but they don't know he is already in The Mist."

"Let's say I believe you. Let's say I am your savior. Now what? You teach me how to use a sword and hope I run into the mythical weapon that can actually kill these monsters?"

"Your journey is not completed yet, Andres. You are not ready to lead an army."

I felt as if I had just gotten off a roller coaster. My head was spinning, and I was on the verge of getting sick.

"So when will I become this hero you are expecting?" I asked.

"You will know when the time is right. The acts that will seal your fate have not taken place yet." His eyes were closed. His mind was traveling through thousands of paths that ended in many different futures. "In the meantime, we save those we can and get them ready," he said.

His face showed hope and certainty. He believed the pieces of this chess game would one day align.

"I still believe you are wrong. I'm not the general that will lead your army, but I can be one of your soldiers. I don't want to die here, and if you can free the slaves, I'm on your side."

"So here is where your path starts." He was pleased.

Part of me wanted to believe he was right. Who doesn't want to be special? Most children want to be superheroes. I certainly did when I was a child. I even let a spider bite me, hoping I would be climbing buildings like Spider-Man. But what Balthazar was talking about was not a silly game. He was proposing that I lead a revolution, and as wonderful as the idea of being chosen sounded, I knew the fate of the slaves could not rest on my shoulders.

I inhaled the aromas of their church one more time because I knew it would be my last. I was certain I was not his worlds walker, but I knew what I could be, and I knew where I needed to start. My mission was extending in front of me like a pathway illuminated by torches. I just had to be brave enough to walk it.

"I need to go back," I said.

He seemed surprised. "If you leave now, you won't come back."

I didn't ask him why. It didn't matter. I had no intention of going back.

"You need me out there. You won't win this war unless all the slaves join your forces when the time is right."

He looked at me, puzzled.

"The slaves we haven't rescued are weak and afraid. They wouldn't survive a second of battle," he replied.

"Maybe . . . or maybe they will give you the edge you need to win this war." My words caught him by surprise.

"It is because of her, right? We can save her if you want. She is strong," he added.

"Claudia is needed in the barracks. She is the force that keeps hope alive. We will organize your first line of defense." The slaves were the key. I knew it in my heart.

"So the first crossroad has been reached, and a decision has been made," he said slowly, loudly. "I will take you back."

He extended his hand, signaling me to grab it.

"Why *worlds walker*?" I asked suddenly. "It is an odd name."

"That is an answer you need to find on your own." Those were the last words I heard before the room surrounding me vanished.

***

When reality reappeared, I was back in the barracks, standing next to my bunk. Guards were throwing people on the floor. They knew Balthazar had been there, but this time, they would not find anybody missing.

As soon as the guards left, the house slaves showed up to dump breakfast into our giant bucket. It had been a rough night for the slaves. Nobody had died, but as always, the jailers had used them as punching bags.

The morning chatter was louder than usual and the voices more agitated and rushed. People were not interested in the food. There were more important matters to address.

"The hidden ones had not visited us in years, and now they have been here twice," Malcolm told a group gathered around him.

The same conversation was taking place in every small group assembled across the quarters. They were afraid. For many slaves, the augurs were monsters from a nightmarish tale passed from generation to generation. They would come in the middle of the night and take the brave and the pure of heart. For the slaves, they were the incarnation of the boogeyman. Now those monsters were real, and their presence was not just frightening, but ominous.

The speculations grew wilder as time passed, and the gasps louder every time someone proposed a new wild theory.

"I heard they use women as reproductive slaves. They get them pregnant over and over until they die," said Malcolm, whose eyes looked wild with enjoyment.

"What do they do with the men?" an anonymous voice in the crowd asked.

"I don't even want to know," the ringleader replied. A chain of sighs and gasps followed his remarks as each person imagined the worst of their fears.

I needed to find Claudia. I had to talk to her before I shared what I had learned with anybody else. I was not going to tell her the crazy prophecy that put me at the center of the augurs' plan, but I was excited to bring her hope. A revolution was brewing, and we had a chance to be part of it. We ought to be ready when the augurs' army launched their attack.

I didn't feel invincible. I just felt ready to sacrifice it all in the name of freedom. I wasn't naive; the chances of dying before even throwing a first punch were real. However, I accepted that.

I thought of my brothers, of the many times I heard of them risking their lives in the name of their beliefs without thinking twice. Growing up, I thought their gift was knowing no fear, but later on, I learned that courage was not just facing the Taliban in the mountains of Afghanistan. Courage is also struggling with adversity and arising victorious. My brothers were not heroic because they were ready to die, but because they were ready to live no matter what was thrown at them.

The day Dani came back from Afghanistan was when I discovered the real meaning of heroism. We were informed a week earlier that he had lost both his legs while fighting in the mountains. The news devastated my parents.

At the hospital, when we were allowed to see him, he greeted us with a big smile.

"I'll be ok," he said, and before my parents had any chance of pouring tears over his chest, he disarmed them with one sentence.

"I am alive. Thirty-five percent lighter, according to my doctor, but breathing. Can we celebrate that?"

That is what made him brave. It wasn't the fact that he fought until he didn't have legs to stand on. His will to survive and push through his shitty circumstance with a smile on his face was what made him courageous. I was ready to follow his example.

As always, Claudia was surrounded by people sharing their problems. They hovered around her like bees waiting for their queen's attention. She had a special gift for making people feel better without downplaying their struggle. The same way she had done it with me. She would talk people off the ledge with nothing but the truth. We were slaves, our lives sucked, but jumping into the abyss of misery was not the answer. The truth was, there was no solution to our circumstances, and we had to learn to live with that. Of course, I no longer agreed with her views, but I still admired her tough-but-caring nature.

Before I got a chance to talk to her, the guards were there to escort us to the field. I rushed to stand behind her like I did most days.

"We need to talk," I whispered.

"I saw him taking you," she responded without turning her head.

A tingling alarm of anxiety rang inside me. If Claudia had seen me leaving, there was a good chance others had as well.

"They can be our way out of here," I said.

"There is no way out of here, Andres. Whatever they said to you, they are lying." She was interrupted by a slap across her face that sounded like gunfire.

She stumbled into me, struggling to keep her footing.

"Shut up!" the guard barked, looking me in the eyes.

The veins on my neck rose. My fists tensed, and my eyes burned with rage. I looked at her face, and the marks of his colossal fingers made me lose all sense of reality. I was ready to launch a kamikaze attack that would cost me my life. I didn't care.

Then I felt Claudia's hand on me. Her eyes were pleading, her expression fearful. My head was then clear.

Have you gone insane? I thought, feeling a combination of frustration and embarrassment. I took a deep breath and let the subtle pressure of her palm guide my huffing chest to its resting position.

"Feeling brave again?" the guard mocked me. "I can arrange another private session with the master. I heard you enjoyed the last one." He laughed.

I kept my gaze down and my lips sealed. I knew that any answer would result in punishment. The guard knew how to hurt me. His monstrous brain had figured out that hitting Claudia was a better way to keep me under control.

He walked away tall and proud. He had shown me who was in charge.

The events of the morning played in my head on a torturing loop all day. I was like Alex in *A Clockwork Orange*, with my eyes held open by specula, witnessing my foolish behavior and Claudia's face begging me to stop.

I dragged the weight of my guilt back into the barracks. Feelings that I had forgotten in the midst of my egotistical drunkenness came back with the fury of old enemies. The air was entering and leaving my body in an accelerated pace that had my heart racing. Drops of sweat, cold as hail, made their way down my forehead, leaving hurtful trails all over my face. I was melting into a puddle of anxiety.

Claudia rushed to the back of the room. She didn't want to deal with me. As weak as I was feeling, I knew I had to follow her. There were not enough words to say how sorry I was, but I had to apologize. I also needed her to hear my story. I knew it was important.

"I am sorry. I don't know what else to say," I said once I caught up with her.

She looked at me with so much anger that my soul hurt. Then she started walking away.

"Claudia, please . . ." I couldn't finish. The knot in my throat stopped my words from coming out.

"I can't do this, Andres," she said while looking away. "You are a good person, but you are losing it, and I can't put my life in danger for you." I tried to find her eyes, but she kept avoiding me. Then her voice got louder. "They know you care about me! So now I am a target. I have not done a thing to enrage them, and now my life is at risk." Her eyes landed on mine, and there was nothing but resentment in them.

She was right. Even if from now on I kept my distance from her, she was in danger. I had turned her into a bargaining chip. She was now the reins the guards would pull when they needed to tame me. I had made a fatal mistake, and she was the one to pay for it.

"Claudia, I know I made you a target, now your life is at risk more than it was before I came here. And to make things worse, your fate rests on my ability to be a good, quiet servant."

"Can you do that for me?" she said, still talking through her teeth.

"No. I can't."

She looked at me with her mouth half-open. Too mad and too surprised to articulate what her heart was feeling.

"I love you too much to let you die here," I continued. "I can promise you I'll be smarter. I can assure you I will not let my impulses get the best of me, but I will not stop until I find us a way out of here."

"You have gone insane!" She walked away. I followed her.

"Claudia, I am not crazy, please just . . ." I grabbed her arm.

Steve shoved me against a bunk bed before I had any time to react. The wood hit my spine, and pain shot all the way to the base of my skull.

"Leave her alone!" He had been listening, and I knew what part of the conversation had made him snap.

I pushed his chest with all my strength and sent him a couple of steps back. His fist flew and landed under my left eye. The room flickered in front of me, but that didn't stop my fists. I felt his skin pressing against his bones and heard his deep moan.

Fingered tentacles grabbed me from behind and started dragging me away from him. I saw him struggling to charge in my direction, but another group of men was holding him back.

"I am ok, let me go, I'm all right!" I said as I stopped struggling.

The men waited a couple of seconds to make sure I was serious and then let me go. A few feet away from me, Steve was free as well.

"Let's talk," Claudia said, not looking at me and walking toward Steve.

If I'd had the power to read auras, I was sure hers would have been bullfighter red.

I sat on the floor, looking up at them on the bed. Steve was avoiding my gaze. He was there just because she had asked him, but if it were up to him, he would be beating my face like a ceremonial drum.

"Tell us what you learned, Andres." She gestured for me to start.

"They call themselves augurs," I started. I waited for some reaction but got nothing but blank stares. "They were the rulers' advisors for many centuries until the eilifts started growing. Slavery came right after the first eilift field, and that is when the augurs rebelled against the kingdom."

"I don't understand how the flowers and the slaves connect," Steve said.

"The flowers make our captors immortal. But to stay that way, they need an increasing amount of eilifts every time," I answered.

"So the hidden ones . . . the augurs, they are not immortal?" asked Claudia.

"No, they refuse to consume the flower," I answered.

"Why?"

"The flower makes those who consume it evil."

Claudia just nodded, an unconvinced expression still framing her face.

"I can't prove that they are the good guys, but I believe them when they say they want to end this nightmare. I think they are against slavery, and that's all that matters to us, right? I mean, why do we care who rules this world after we leave?"

Something I said hit a chord. I saw a softening in their faces. Steve's shoulders descended a couple of inches, and I knew then that at least some of my words were getting through.

I shared every detail I was able to recall except my prophetic role in the augurs' plan. I described the augurs' church. I beamed when I talked about the faces of the liberated slaves. I described the smells and the welcoming demeanor of the chubby woman I encountered. But Claudia and Steve were not impressed with my fairy tale.

"We have a common goal," I concluded. "They want slavery to end and to overthrow the evil rulers. They are on our side, which should give us hope." I leaned closer to their faces. I wanted my faith to reach them.

Steve got up. "Even if they're telling the truth, we'll be nothing but their meat shields. They will put us in front of their troops on the battlefield, and let us get slaughtered while they march to victory. I won't die fighting their war. Sorry, Andres, but you, as always, are just trying to get us killed." I didn't have an answer for him, and he didn't wait for one either.

I looked at Claudia with begging eyes. The fury in her face was gone.

"Look around you, Andres. Do you see warriors?" The sadness in her voice was as deep as the misery surrounding us. "Most of them are sick and weak. Most of them are nothing but human shells performing tasks as if they were rituals."

"We can change that. We can exercise, become stronger—"

"Stop." She cut me off. "They keep us hungry and weak for a reason, Andres. Have you noticed that the healing water closes wounds but doesn't heal illnesses? They know what they are doing."

"I didn't say it was going to be easy. But we can try. Do you want to die as a slave?"

"I want to live. Don't try to shame me for that!"

"This is not living."

"Yes, it is." Her words were firm. "We may not like it, but it is living. We may live in misery, but we live. I am ok with that." She rose. "You can't just become a hero and expect to drag us all into some holy war. Not long ago you were just a scared guy wishing he was dead. Now, all of a sudden, you want to be a general." Her words stabbed like a knife.

The conversation was over. She left me there stranded in a sea of conflicting thoughts. She was right on every count. I knew that. But there was a stronger force within me, clearing a path that I knew headed toward freedom. There was a way out, I could feel it in my bones, and the augurs were the key.

Many times, Grandma Elisa had said to me that faith was the strongest fuel you could inject into your soul.

"It is like what they put in rockets. It can take you all the way to heaven. That's powerful, *mijo*." Her eyes would look so deep into my soul that I felt embarrassed, as if I were standing naked in front of her. "Faith in God and faith in yourself, Andres, even if you are standing in hell."

Until then I had never gotten my hands on that kind of energy. I didn't know what the power of believing in the impossible felt like, but now the feeling was there, rooted in my heart like an ancient oak—solid and unshakable. My friends' disbelief was not enough to discourage me. I knew it would take time, but one day they would join me.

"So when is this revolution starting?" His voice came from behind me. I had not heard him approaching.

I turned around and saw him standing with the same off-putting appearance I noticed in him the first time. Lakay was a kid scared to death but brave enough not to let that stop him from jumping into a fight.

"You were spying on us?"

"Anybody who gives a shit could hear you. It's not like there are any walls. Lucky you, most people ran out of shits to give a long time ago," he said, looking smug.

"I don't know when they will attack. But I believe we need to be ready to act on short notice."

His eyes revealed little. I couldn't tell if he believed my words or not, or if he thought it was all nonsense. He stood there for a minute or so, letting the awkwardness settle.

"Claudia says you are not a creep, just dumb."

"She's right, I guess," I said with a smile.

"I can see that." He scratched his nose and looked around like he was searching for someone. "We are straight, then, and if your revolution is happening, count me in. I won't die in this shithole."

He walked to his bunk bed, kicking the floor every couple of steps as if an invisible ball were rolling in front of him.

***

The next morning, I sprang into a sitting position with the alarming feeling that I had overslept. With my surroundings still unfocused, I rushed to the entrance of the slave quarters, hoping to at least grab a bite before the guards showed up. The food was in its usual place, but it wasn't swarming with bodies around it. Two guys were sitting with their legs crossed, facing each other, scooping and eating goo with an odd calm.

Everybody else seemed to be taking their time. There were small groups of people chatting and even laughing. A group of younger men, led by Lakay, was doing push-ups as if a little boot-camp workout was the most reasonable thing.

I did an entire 360 searching for a glimpse of normality but came back empty-handed. The slave quarters had turned into a lively town square.

"It is our day off," said Claudia, trying to fluff the raw wool we called a mattress. She wasn't having much luck. "It happens at random, sometimes ten days apart, sometimes a month. I have no idea why."

"How do you know you are getting the day off, then?"

"Because the guards don't come after breakfast. You know we get minutes to swallow that disgusting thing before we leave for the fields. Well, when we notice the food has been sitting there for more than just a couple of minutes, then we know the guards won't come back until the next day."

Claudia was in a good mood, like everybody else. She smiled at me, letting me know that, at least for the day, we were ok.

"Lakay told me you talked to him."

"It took a lot of work convincing that kid you were not a perverted creep. He did not like you, let me tell you."

"I appreciate it, thanks."

"I didn't want him spreading rumors. The last thing we needed was people believing their hero is a pervert."

Blood colored my face when I heard the word *hero*. She looked at me and continued.

"That is why I can't let you get revolutionary ideas in your head, Andres. They can think you are a hero, but if they start thinking you are also their savior, they will follow you. Then they'll die beside you." There was nothing but concern in her voice.

It was not the time to start a new argument. The day off was the first hint of happiness I had seen in that place. I was not about to ruin it for Claudia or anybody else.

"So what do people do on this glorious holiday," I said, attempting to lighten the mood.

"Most times just rest and chat, but today I think we have an overachiever." She pointed at Lakay and his group.

"I didn't ask him to—"

"I know, don't worry about it." Claudia motioned for me to join her. "You know what would be awesome to do on a day off?" Her face was painted with the memory of a happier time. "Go to a fancy restaurant and have a big piece of steak." She closed her eyes, and I could almost see the images of juicy and tender sirloins dancing in her head.

The sound of my laugh felt invigorating. I scanned the room and was hit by a revelation: even in hell, joy can find a way.

Claudia was talking about some of her favorite restaurants in Miami when the room went silent. We stood up and joined the eyes of the rest of the surprised and scared slaves. Roman, escorted by two guards, was standing at the entrance of the room.

He looked like a god in front of a crowd of lepers.

CHAPTER 10

Roman and his guards escorted me from the slave quarters through a series of bright corridors filled with paintings and sculptures dedicated to the queen.

"Do you care about sports? I can tell you who won the Super Bowl if you are interested. I don't understand the appeal of human sports. The whole running-behind-a-ball thing seems just odd and a little barbaric."

"Where are you taking me?" I said.

"It is a surprise, but I promise you'll love it."

"Last time you told me that, you sold me into slavery," I snapped at him.

"If it makes you feel better, I did not make a penny from you."

I didn't answer. I just wanted to find a sharp object and drive it deep into his throat.

Roman's outfit stood out like a careless anachronism in the halls of the castle. His freshly pressed dark-blue shirt embraced his body all the way to his waist, where it disappeared into a pair of slim white pants, the kind that lure your eyes to the crotch no matter how hard you try not to look. The small heels on his short camel-skin boots made a shallow sound that echoed all through the chambers every time they hit the stone floor. If someone had said he had flown straight from Milan's fashion week, nobody would have doubted it.

I hated myself for the mixed feelings his presence sparked in me. From the very beginning, I felt an unusual energy flowing between us, a pulling force that crippled my capacity to make rational decisions. *You are attracted to him.* The thought popped into my brain like an unwelcomed guest, and it disgusted me.

We made it to the main hall of the castle. Its size and brightness surprised me once again.

"Beautiful, isn't it?" he said as if reading my mind.

I remained quiet. I kept marching next to him with my eyes fixed on the pathway ahead.

Roman continued giving me updates on pop culture and politics, like a loud television you couldn't turn off.

"Roman, please tell me what is going on."

His ocean-deep eyes landed with fury on mine. He stopped and faced me with a puzzled expression. Then his right hand was on my throat and my back was hitting the wall behind me. The air in my lungs was extinguished as my chest convulsed, begging for oxygen to return.

"I like this new Andres. The determination is alluring, but right now you are annoying me." His hand squeezed a little tighter. My surroundings were blurring.

When he let me go, I fell to the ground. I inhaled air like a hungry animal while attempting to stand again.

We arrived in what looked like a luxury suite. As soon as we entered the room, he guided me to the bathroom.

Heavy maroon curtains covered the walls, which gave the place the appearance of a theater stage. The lighting was soft but abundant. The whole scene seemed to be colored in sepia, like an old photograph brought to life.

There were many little objects scattered on wooden vanities and plush benches, all of them painted by the moody light emanating from the red orbs.

"Get in there." Roman pointed at the silver tub in the middle of the room.

"What do you want from me, Roman?"

He smiled. "I want you to take those filthy rags off and get in the tub." He pointed again as if I had not seen the object the first time.

I took my clothes off with hesitation. My face was burning, and a numbing sense of exposure came over me. I walked toward the tub, hunching over as much as I could, as if my bending spine could protect me from his eyes.

"You are amusing," Roman said with a sigh.

The water covered me up to my shoulders. I looked down at my distorted body, and somehow the transparent veil made me feel safer.

"Wash yourself." He threw at me a porous and light object that looked like a piece of volcanic rock.

As I rubbed the stone against my skin, thin foam started rising. The smell of lavender and crisp air rose into my nostrils. I sighed as a velvety fluid blanket embraced me.

The grimace on his face was an unnerving sign of what I thought was coming. There were not many reasons why he would like me to be clean. I was certain he was not taking me to a party; not one that I would enjoy, anyway.

"Is the water warm enough for you?" Roman's hand submerged until it touched my knee. His fingers lingered and then left.

He walked around the room, pretending to be distracted by picking up brushes and containers that he played with for a second or two before moving on. I could sense his eyes on me.

"You know I almost let you go that night?" he asked.

"Before I opened the door, when you told me I didn't have to go to the party?"

"Yes."

"Why?"

"I am still wondering that myself." There was an odd sense of honesty in his voice.

Roman stopped in front of the tub, facing me with an unreadable expression.

"Stand up . . . and don't make me repeat myself."

I did as he said.

"Stand straight. I want to take a good look at you."

I closed my eyes and stood straight.

"There is something odd about you, Andres. It is more than the fact that you are a fine specimen of the human race." He started circling the tub, his eyes piercing my skin with every look. "Look at your body. After months of slavery and starvation, you are still as strong as one of the bulls in Pamplona." I kept my eyes closed, listening to the sound of his boots. "And then there is this feeling, this connection, that I'm sure you sense too." Each one of his steps made me shiver. "Tell me, what do you feel for me, Andres?"

"Hate." The word escaped me, but I wasn't sorry.

"I know it is a lot more complicated than that," he said with conviction.

Roman walked to a closet and took out a towel and a new slave uniform.

"Get dressed," he said as he placed the clothing on a bench and exited the room.

Outside, in the main suite, there was a table, two chairs, and an entire feast waiting for me. The smell of the braised meat reminded me of my mother's kitchen. Cumin and paprika mixed with the pine-like smell of fresh rosemary. The juices in my mouth started flowing free and eager, demanding to taste every piece of meat, fruit, and vegetable displayed in front of me.

Next to the table there was also a young man in a white uniform, holding an ornate wooden pitcher. It was Carlos.

"Take a seat." Roman's face was inviting in the same deceiving way it had been the night I met him.

I was not about to disobey. I knew what his fury could do, but I was curious too. I wanted to understand what twisted plan was brewing in his brain. Sometimes the only way to learn the habits of the devil is to hold his hand and take a walk in his burning garden.

"Carlos, please pour wine for our guest."

Carlos obeyed without responding. His brown eyes had the dead stare of those whose brains have been washed clean. His hair was cut tight, and his nails were manicured. His skin smelled like what I imagined was the aroma of Havana during a summer night—tropical fruits and fine tobacco. He was Roman's toy, and without a doubt, he was Lidia's son.

"You brought me here to have dinner?" I asked.

"You are quite an ungrateful prick, Andres. You are lucky I like you." He winked at me.

He started eating with his hands.

Roman looked into my eyes, squinting as if he were trying to read a book written with tiny letters.

"I heard you got yourself a girlfriend."

My head sprang up when I heard his words. He continued, "Don't feel embarrassed. It is entirely reasonable and understandable."

"I don't have a girlfriend. I have made friends, if that is what you mean."

"I have to admit, when I met you, I thought you were queer. I mean, closeted and still trying to convince yourself you were not, but queer none the less. I also figured you would stop pretending here. It is not like you are going to disappoint your daddy or anything." He was mocking me. He knew exactly which words would hurt the most.

"You just wished I was gay. Sorry to disappoint you," I answered angrily.

"You haven't," he said cheerfully. "Just don't get her pregnant. We don't forbid love. But if she gets pregnant, she and the bastard will be killed." He savored the last words as if committing that murder was something he was looking forward to doing.

I ate in silence while Roman launched into a scattered monologue about the hypocrisy of human society and its insistence on hiding its true nature behind the mask of morality and the common good.

"We are not enslaving you. You were all slaves already. You just don't admit it. Here we just make it more obvious." Those were his final remarks. Then he called the guards and ordered them to take me back. Before I left, he cupped my face with his hands.

"I should have let Ash kill you. Now you are just another one of my problems," he said. Then he let me go.

***

I was welcomed back to the dungeon by chilly stares and resentful looks. My clean clothing stood out like an orchid in a filthy swamp. I became conscious of my smell, the color of my cheeks, and the natural glow of my well-rested and well-fed body.

I kept my head down as I walked toward my bunk. The food was gone. Soon everybody would be in bed.

I should have known that Roman's actions were not random. He knew the effect my new uniform and the smell of wine on my breath would have. He knew there would be resentment among the other slaves. At no point did I think kindness had inspired his intentions, but until I went back to my prison, I had no idea what the implications would be.

"What was that all about?" Claudia had caught up to me.

"I have no idea. He made me bathe, change, and then he fed me," I answered, full of embarrassment.

"It sounds like a great first date. Are you calling him back?" There wasn't a hint of humor in her voice, just pure and cutting sarcasm.

"Don't do that, please. You know I didn't ask for this."

"It doesn't look like you resisted it too much either."

"Claudia, why are you upset? You are the one who asked me not to do anything stupid. Would it be less upsetting for you if I had bruises covering my face?"

As she walked away, she mumbled something that sounded like a "maybe." I didn't have the mental strength to go after her.

CHAPTER 11

I knew I had not done anything wrong. I had not betrayed anybody or sold myself for any price. But still, I felt guilty. I enjoyed that bath, and I liked that meal. Was that wrong? Was I a traitor? Claudia and the rest of the slaves believed so, and at that point, their perception was all that mattered to me.

The morning came, and it was clear my offense was greater than I thought. Hostile looks and mumbled nasty words followed me as I walked toward the food.

"I thought you would still be full from last night," said Margaret, blocking my way.

I didn't answer. Margaret was a nice lady when she wanted to be, but she could also be a mean enemy if you rubbed her the wrong way. I walked back to my bed and waited there until it was time to go to the fields.

I could understand the initial upset, but the overall reaction seemed exaggerated. I was forced to leave. I did what Roman demanded because my life was at stake. I thought everybody would understand that.

I didn't even bother standing close to Claudia or Steve. I lined up last and followed the group in silence. When we arrived at the fields, I kept my distance from the men and women surrounding me.

Human nature survives even in the most inhumane circumstances, I thought.

Just hours before, I had been a hero. People admired my courage. Claudia was afraid I would inspire slaves to revolt. The next day, I was a pariah, a traitor who had dared to succumb to the temptation of our captors.

We love to create heroes, but we love even more to see them fall. It makes us feel better about ourselves. We celebrate those who rise to the top because of their virtue, but we hate them for the same reasons. Heroes remind us how complacent and cowardly we all are. They expose us to our inability to change our circumstances, so we are glad when they fail.

The day crawled to an end. I went straight to my bed and lay there with my eyes closed, hoping to sleep and forget the anger brewing in me. I wasn't upset because of the scarlet letter placed on my chest. It was the swiftness of their judgment; it was how natural it felt for all the slaves to hate me without thinking twice.

"They are afraid." Lakay was sitting on the floor next to my bed. "You were a source of hope. They are afraid the master bought you with a shower and a meal."

"That just shows me how little they think of me. A meal and a new uniform are a low price to pay for someone's loyalty," I replied without opening my eyes.

"Is it?"

He had a point. Most people around me had lived in filth for years and hadn't tasted real food since their arrival. For them, I had been awarded the highest possible prize after freedom, and they were positive that such a prize was not free.

"Why are you being nice to me, Lakay?"

"I am not being nice. I am making sure my ticket out of here doesn't change his mind. I know you're doing what you've got to do to survive. I don't judge you, man. They'll get over it."

But the kid was wrong. Weeks went by, and I was still the target of gossip and mistrust. Claudia had warmed up to me. But I could feel a lingering uneasiness when we talked. Something between us had changed, and I had no clue how to fix it. I didn't have the courage to bring it up either. I was happy she was speaking to me, even if the caring inflection in her voice was gone.

During that time, the guards would show up at random hours and take me out of the quarters. Then I would sit in a corridor for a couple of hours until they brought me back. Roman was feeding fuel to the burning mistrust growing around me.

Adding to my problems was Lakay. He and his friends continued their morning exercise routine. As time went by, they became cocky and careless. The guards beat many of them for their acts of defiance, but that didn't stop them.

I talked to him more than once, but the impulses of his youth made him deaf.

"An army of dead men is no good. Tell your guys to lay low," I said over and over, yet he couldn't help himself.

"Man, we need a plan B," he said, waking me up in the middle of the night.

"What are you talking about?"

"Well . . . what if the rest never forgive you and the augurs decide to attack." His eyes kept shifting from one side to another, as if he was afraid of being caught talking to me.

"Lakay, I think you're getting ahead of yourself. Don't do anything stupid, please. We have plenty of time—"

"How do you know that?" he cut me off. "I thought you said this was going down soon." He sounded irritated.

"Just listen to me, keep your guys organized and lay low. That's the plan for now."

"Doesn't sound like a plan to me," he barked and left.

He had a point, though. If I was still serious about joining the augurs' army, I couldn't let Roman win this battle that easily. I had to talk to the slaves and convince them this was a setup. The revolution was going to happen independent of who was mad at me.

"Roman wants to make my life miserable," I told Lidia. "He just enjoys seeing me suffer."

"He doesn't want to make you suffer, Andres. He wants to isolate you. He wants us to hate you, and he wants you to hate us back, so when he offers you a way out of the dungeon, you don't think twice before accepting." Lidia was using her son's story as a cautionary tale.

I talked to Malcolm, Margaret, and some of the other slaves, and even though they believed my story, they were not convinced I would reject the chance of becoming a house slave. After all, I had already accepted Roman's "gifts."

"Do slaves get to say no if they are ordered to serve in the house instead of the fields?" I asked Claudia.

"Only Carlos has been presented with that option, and he was quick to accept. I don't know what would happen if you say no."

"They don't trust me because of something Carlos did." I shook my head in frustration.

"They don't want their hopes shattered and their hearts broken once again. I don't blame them," Claudia responded, giving me a pointed look.

I did my best to win the slaves' trust again, but it wasn't an easy task.

Adding to my problems was Lakay's thoughtless behavior. The more anxious he became, the more reckless he acted. As I expected, his stubborn spirit led him straight into the fists and boots of a group of guards.

Our shift was almost over when Lakay decided to put his basket down and sit on the ground. His chest rose to the sky, full of pride and delusional confidence. His eyes asked for the chance to oppose the system, to emerge as a leader of his tribe.

Before anybody could warn him, three guards were beating him mercilessly. They didn't ask a question or yell an order. They were not in the mood to be bothered by a clueless slave. The sound of boots crushing his bones rang out, but nobody reacted. The usual sound of the eilifts' stems continued rolling through the fields with its sad melody, unaware and unbothered by the drifting life of a young and careless fool.

Blood was pooling next to him, and I noticed his mouth powdered with white crystals. His mind was being tortured in some distant memory while his body was receiving a punishment that could lead nowhere else but to his death.

I should have let him die like everybody else, but I couldn't. Part of me wanted to save the kid, but I also wanted to show the rest that I wasn't a traitor. I wanted them to know that I was not afraid of fighting.

I yelled at the guards, but they didn't acknowledge me. I ran through the fields to where Lakay was lying, but before I could reach him, a guard stopped me in my tracks. I struggled with all my might, but his grip had the firmness of an anaconda. He didn't hurt me, though; he just held me there, as if he was protecting me from myself.

The slaves pretended not to see Lakay's punishment, but they stared at me without hiding their incredulous expressions. The guard was shielding me. That was all they saw.

Lakey's body was spread, lifeless, in a puddle of his blood. The cruel giants left him lying there like a deflated ball that they had gotten tired of playing with. I ran to him as soon as I was free from my captor. I cleaned the snow from his lips and started blowing life into his lungs. My hands pressed against his chest, attempting to revive his heart, but I heard his ribs shattering as the weight of my body leaned on them.

"Come on, man, follow my voice. Come back to us," I whispered.

His eyes were closed and his expression distorted. The pain he had endured was visible in his face like a sinister Halloween mask.

I heard the rolling of the cart climbing the pathway of the field like the carriage of the Grim Reaper approaching in the distance. He was dead, and his transport to the fangs of the fenrirs had arrived.

"Get out of the way." Steve's voice was firm.

"I'll help you," I said in between sobs.

"They want you back there." He pointed toward the guards.

One of the giants was smiling at me, standing right behind Claudia. If I didn't obey, she would pay for it. That was his message, and I knew better than to ignore it.

Lakay's death was on me. Claudia had warned me that spreading revolutionary ideas would do nothing but get people killed, and it had. The kid had believed my words. He thought that a revolt was brewing, and I was the commander that would lead him and his friends to freedom. He was wrong. Believing in me had filled him with an irresponsible sense of invulnerability. My promises were the poison that killed him.

I had never felt that kind of soul-corrupting guilt. In the days that followed, I walked around in a haze, avoiding people at all costs. I didn't care what they thought about me anymore. I was dangerous. Death emanated from me like a contagious disease.

I faded until I became a bad episode in the slaves' memories. I stopped eating every day, and when I did, I would wait until the last minute so few would see me. I stood at the end of the line when they led us to the field and went straight to my bed when we returned.

Soon enough I had forgotten the better version of myself that I had become for an ephemeral second.

Claudia and Steve stayed away, and it hurt. But at the same time, I was glad they were done with me. Becoming a faceless blue uniform in the crowd would have been a lot harder if I'd still had their friendship.

***

The next day off—maybe a month after Lakay's death—Roman showed up again.

His guards dragged me screaming, crying, and cursing up the stairs.

Roman had engineered the entire situation. He had taken everything away from me, and now he was there just to finish the job. I was going to die, and nobody would care.

I stopped struggling. There was no point.

"I want to show you something," said Roman.

He was pensive. His usual flamboyant tone was absent.

We walked through hallways and galleries without saying a word. The drumming of his shoes was the lone sound following us for what seemed like hours.

We arrived at a spacious room with dark wood walls and marble floors the color of volcanic ash. The ceiling extended to a point so high it seemed infinite, giving the space a strange outdoors feeling. Paintings of the queen covered the lustrous walls. Her goddess-like figure was depicted performing the most varied tasks. Most of them were violent. Many of them involved her spilling someone's blood.

Roman turned to face me. He wore an unreadable expression. It was like standing in front of a giant dog. I couldn't tell if he was ready to jump on me and rip me to pieces or grab my face and lick me.

"Which one would you rather?" he asked.

I was confused by the question. But then it dawned on me. "You can read my thoughts," I answered.

"Not all the time," he said, looking away, making it clear he was not planning on elaborating on the subject.

"Where are we?" I asked.

"It is called the Gallery of Remembrance. Ash built it to honor my mother."

I looked at the pictures one more time. The woman decorating every inch of the castle with her heroic and sadistic actions, the queen, was Roman's mother.

"That would make you Prince Roman," I replied.

"No, it doesn't. Many years ago she decided I was unworthy of the crown." Bitterness coated every single word he said. "You see, I am a catcher, which means there is human DNA somewhere in my bloodline. There is no worse disgrace than that. A filthy descendant of animals could never rule this kingdom." His fist tightened, and his shoulders tensed. He was not talking to me, though; he was spitting the words back into his mother's face.

"Catchers are part human?" I asked, finding the fact hard to believe.

"We are not. One of our ancestors was. That is what gives us the ability to cross back and forth into your world. No other creature has that power." He sounded proud.

"You can also read minds?"

"I can read yours, only sometimes, though. I don't know why." He looked at me, mystified. "I noticed it the night I met you. At first, I wasn't sure of it. I thought you were so pathetic and predictable it was easy to know what you were feeling. But as the night went by, it became apparent I was able to sense some of your feelings and hear some of your thoughts."

He started walking around the room, stopping in front of paintings and scrutinizing them as if he was searching for clues.

"They erased me from royal history, you know? She removed my face from every piece of art in the kingdom."

I was not prepared for a heart-to-heart with the architect of all my misery. What did he expect from me? Empathy? Did he want me to say I was sorry he would not become king because his mother was a sadistic racist?

"I'm not asking for your sympathy, Andres. I don't need anything from you," he said, rolling his eyes. "I brought you here because you became a problem, and it is time that I take care of it."

"Why don't you just kill me, then?" There was no defiance in my words, just plain curiosity.

"Because dead heroes become martyrs, and martyrs inspire revolutions. The last thing we need here is a slaves' revolt." He continued walking.

"I'm far from a hero, Roman. They hate me—"

"They don't," he interrupted me. "At least not entirely. Many of them still hope for you to rise from the ashes of disgrace. If I kill you, I will confirm you were not a traitor." His hands adorned his words in that dramatic way he loved so much.

"Then what?" I replied. "You keep taking me on field trips until the slaves truly hate me?"

He laughed wholeheartedly.

"The way to kill a hero is not by ending his life, Andres. You first take away his people, those who elevated him to glory. Then you take away his confidence. And then, you kill his soul." His wicked smiled shone in front of my face.

"I'm so sick of your ridiculous speeches! There is no soul to kill, Roman. I've been dead inside since the day you brought me here." The room felt hot, my blood was boiling.

"And there it is again." He put his finger on my chest and pushed hard toward my heart. "You think your soul is dead, but it is just numb. And when I tell you that the guards were just waiting for an opportunity to kill one of your friends, your thirst for revenge will possess you and your veins will explode with pulsing rage." His finger stayed there, pushing harder. The beat of my heart was pumping on his fingertip.

"Why Lakay? Why not kill Claudia? If you really wanted to hurt me, you knew she was the one."

He shook his head. He was enjoying sharing the details of his master plan and realizing how clueless I was. "Because that would have made you angry, not sad. Sorrow erodes the spirit. Sadness turns the fertile soil of a hero's heart into a desert. Anger, on the other hand, replaces your blood with fire. Anger transforms the howls of your wounded heart into roars."

My eyes searched for something to grab. I wanted to hurt him, I wanted to beat him until his skin split and his filthy blood fouled the immaculate floors. He knew what I was thinking, but he didn't care, and neither did I.

He grabbed my hand and guided me deeper into the chamber. I tried to free myself, but his grip was unwavering. We stopped in front of a painting as wide as the ten-foot wall holding it.

Ulda had a sword in one hand and the head of a man in the other. Blood was dripping from his severed neck into a bed of eilifts. The flowers sparked like a guiding star. There were people around her, cheering. Their faces twisted between euphoria and wrath. The death of that man was desired and celebrated.

"He is what you can call the father of the eilifts. He was human, and his blood brought eternal life into The Mist," Roman said.

"A slave?" I asked.

"A king. Ulda's king." He smiled at my surprised face. "Ulda's first and only husband was a human. It was a different time. There were portals connecting our worlds, and delegations from many kingdoms would cross from one to another, exchanging knowledge and magic."

"What happened?"

"Ulda realized humans are nothing but unworthy animals." He made a purposeful pause. He wanted the words to sink into me. "King Leif saw in Ulda's love the chance to expand his kingdom, but she was not part of his plan. He had a human queen waiting on the other side." Roman's grin was full of amusement. "So he started sneaking troops into our world. He was preparing an invasion. He thought his weapons were enough to defeat our magic."

"I guess your mother found out."

"She did. And you can see how that ended for him."

"He was your father?"

"No, I was adopted by Ulda a long time after his death," he said, letting my hand go and touching the head bleeding in the painting. He grabbed my hand again and walked me to the furthermost end of the room.

In front of a wide window, there were two chairs facing two heavy black curtains. We sat next to each other as two guards flanked both sides of the frame. I could hear unintelligible noises coming from the other side. It sounded like muffled prayers. Like the hums of a crowded church in the distance.

Roman closed his eyes and pointed his face toward the ceiling in ecstasy. The murmurs were music for him. A symphony he adored and followed with the gentle sway of his head.

Without opening his eyes, he swiped the air, giving the guards the signal to reveal what awaited on the other side.

That was his surprise, what he wanted to show me.

The curtains opened. I shut my eyes, dazzled by the reflected light of the eilift field. My ears adjusted before my eyes. The prayers were cries and wails arising from the mouths of humans.

Naked bodies tied to stakes spread through the field. Men, women, and children stood there immobilized and helpless. Their eyes were begging for mercy while their mouths erupted in pain.

"King Leif's blood, mixed with the dust in the fields of pain, birthed the first eilifts. It was instant. As soon as his blood touched the ground, the little flowers started sprawling." The shrieks grew louder, and so did Roman's voice.

Dread traveled through my veins like venom. My eyes kept skipping between Roman and the vile spectacle in front of me. I watched with horror as a group of women dressed in ragged white tunics walked around feeding white powder to the hostages. That was the reason for their frightening screams. Their brains were being tortured as much as their bodies.

"You see, the queen knew they were a gift from the gods. The almighties were celebrating Ulda's wisdom and bravery." For the first time, there was pride in his voice when pronouncing his mother's name.

I was having trouble breathing. The walls seemed to be moving toward me and the air thinning. I wanted to run. I wanted to jump into the field and free them. I wanted to grab the children in my arms and shield them from the monsters.

"We tried to water them, but they kept wilting. Then it became evident that they fed on human blood." His words had the weight of a death sentence.

I looked at the meadow in a panic. I knew what was coming.

"The king's men were the first offering to the flowers of life. From then on, every time the sun moves we present a new gift to our source of eternal life."

I looked at the stakes spread like tombs on a snowy cemetery. The women in tunics were gone. An icy silence that lasted a second and an eternity at the same time broke the unnerving noise beating in my ears. And then, the growls started building like the sound of a landslide dragging death and destruction down a mountain.

A pack of fenrirs raced into the field. The terrified humans screamed, but their noises were drowned out by the sounds of bones crushing and flesh ripping. The animals tore the bodies to pieces with just one bite and then feasted on their flesh with the voracity of the famished. Howling and snarling replaced the cries. Blood ran, irrigating the thirsty flowers that shined brighter when touched by the velvety crimson river. The souls of the victims were soaking the roots of the eilifts while the fenrirs devoured their last remains.

"There is no light like the light of the eilifts," Roman said, as if he was praying.

Then I saw him. Front and center, tied to a stake like all the others. One of his arms was already missing. His face wore indescribable pain. I mumbled his name as tears started pouring from my eyes. "Jorge." My brother was one of the sacrifices.

Bile rose from my stomach to my throat. Its sour taste overwhelmed my mouth. I was dripping sweat as cold as the Arctic while my vision became a tunnel from which I could only see Roman's eyes.

"Please understand, Andres, your brother is serving a higher purpose. His life is perpetuating the existence of the race that one day will liberate your kind from the world of hypocrisy where you live. We can share that honor with your mother, your father, and the rest of your family. Or you can extinguish those delusions of grandeur and become an advocate for obedience and servitude. I will honor your wishes." His eyes stabbed my soul until it lay lifeless in front of him.

I was paralyzed by pain and horror. Jorge was being devoured by monsters. His blood was running through the meadow, feeding the flowers I would be picking the next day.

"I'll do whatever you want." The words escaped my mouth.

"Perfect! But don't take offense in the fact that I can't just take your word for it. I want public displays of submission and humility. I want you to take every punishment—and believe me, there will be plenty—with your head down and beg for mercy in front of your fellow slaves. I want them to know that their hero is nothing but another coward."

I nodded.

"When I'm convinced of your submissiveness, I will pay you another visit and I will offer you the chance to become a house slave. You will accept without hesitation. If you don't, you will witness the violent and gruesome death of the rest of your family."

CHAPTER 12

The nightmares became so real I stopped sleeping. The face of my mother screaming in agony as the fenrirs dismembered her fragile body flashed in my brain like a warning sign on a highway.

In the darkness of the slave quarters, I wished death would find me and free me from my guilt. It was just a matter of time until the load on my shoulders became heavier. I knew what hell would look like for me. I would walk among the flames, hunched over with the burden of those I had wronged. From the puddle of self-pity and misery where I was sitting, I could see the faces of those sentenced to death by my thoughtless actions.

It had been days since my encounter with Roman. I assumed the rest of the slaves thought I'd had another nice date with the oppressor. I didn't care to clarify, and they didn't bother to ask me.

I continued with my new routine. I would eat every other day, do my job in silence, and stay away from everybody. I didn't know if that would be enough to keep my family safe, but I didn't know what else to do.

Roman's words kept swirling in my head: "Become an advocate for obedience and servitude." I didn't know how to do that except by staying out of the spotlight and taking my punishments with resignation.

"She is hurting." Steve's voice manifested like a spirit next to my bed.

It was the middle of the night. I had not heard someone addressing me in so many weeks I was surprised by how warming it felt. I rolled over and looked at him. I didn't get up.

"She knows something happened to you, and she feels guilty for letting the other slaves treat you the way they have," Steve continued.

He was such a strange character. He acted like he hated me most of the time, but he was always there trying to help me when I was at my lowest. I knew Claudia was his concern, and he was talking to me because of her. But why? We both knew each had feelings for her. Still he was there letting me know she didn't hate me.

"Why are you telling me this, Steve?"

"Because I can't stand to see her suffer."

"You love her."

"You know the answer to that. It is obvious to anybody with eyes and a half-functioning brain." We both smiled. It was true, and it was funny. "Listen, Andres, none of us will ever have her. Claudia is not the kind of woman who needs a man or who lets her feelings get in the way of her survival."

I sat up and saw him shifting his weight from one leg to another.

"What did they do to you?" he asked.

"They killed my soul."

"A soul cannot be killed, Andres. Only someone without one would think such thing is possible. They wounded you. They scared you, but your soul is still there."

I wished I had spent less time fighting with Steve and more time getting to know him. Even though his approach was brusque, he was always trying to make people feel better. He wasn't great at it, but he tried.

"Those are profound words, Steve."

"Before this life, I was in the business of fixing injured souls." He grinned with so much yearning in his face.

"Were you a shrink?"

"A priest."

That came as a surprise. Since our first encounter, I had thought Steve had been a football player or a club bouncer. Priest was a shocking revelation.

"How does a priest end up in a place like this?" I said, perplexed by the idea.

"I wasn't a great priest. I mean, I was passionate and dedicated to my job. I was not good at following the rules. I had issues with that vow of chastity."

I laughed, and he joined me.

"So a female catcher took you," I said.

"Something like that. We can share life stories some other day, Andres. I'm tired. Just promise me you'll talk to Claudia."

"I will," I said, even though I had no idea how I would get the strength to do it or what I would say.

I decided I wouldn't tell her what I had seen. The reality of The Mist was much more vicious than anybody could imagine, and there was no reason for her to carry the weight of that revelation.

I approached Claudia with caution. I wasn't sure what my opening sentence was going to be.

"I'm sorry," she said as soon as I was close enough.

I didn't want to cry in front of her, so I held my breath for a couple of seconds before answering.

"You don't need to apologize for anything . . ."

"Yes, I do. I let my anger and fear hurt you. I should have known better. I know you better. I know you would never do something to hurt me or anybody else here." Her voice was breaking, and I knew she hated it.

"Why are we both trying not to cry?" I said, smiling.

"Because we are idiots who don't know how to express emotions. You should know that by now," she said amid cries and laughs.

She walked toward me and buried her head in my chest. I held her there with my chin resting on her head and my heart beating with the speed of a racehorse.

She stepped back and cleared her tears.

"What did they do to you, Andres?"

"Roman threatened with killing my family if I continued challenging them," I said and felt chills just by saying the words. "He said he will test me. He will make me prove that all vestiges of rebellion are gone."

She probably wanted to say "I told you so," but she didn't. She had warned me more than once about the consequences of playing hero. I just refused to listen.

Claudia decided to change the subject and started telling me about the gossip. Nobody blamed me for Lakay's death. The slaves thought he had asked for it, but they also thought I was trading information and favors for "luxuries."

"What kind of favors?" I said, annoyed.

"The exact kind you are thinking. You wouldn't be the first, believe me."

I didn't know what was most appalling, the fact that I had fallen from hero to whore or the fact that such an abomination had happened before.

"So what now?" I asked.

"Now we go back to before the augurs filled your head with nonsense. The others will forgive, and Ash and Roman will forget about you when they realize you are not a threat."

I wasn't sure that last part was true.

***

I could sense the danger in the air the moment I walked into the fields. It was in their looks. The guards were up to something, and that was always bad news for us.

The cries of slaves punished for no reason soon started.

"You have become too comfortable!" Their boss walked around screaming at us. "You forgot your place in this kingdom. You are nothing but worthless farm animals!"

There was such rage in his voice. His hate was palpable, and it manifested in random attacks on those closer to him.

He approached me. His hand slammed into my chest with such force I fell to the ground and slid backward a couple of inches.

"You initiated this!" he yelled.

It was starting. Roman had instructed the guards to push me. To test my limits and make sure my head was always bowing.

His colossal fingers lifted me by my collar until my eyes were right in front of his. I looked down.

"Look at me, slave! I want to see your eyes when you answer."

I didn't know what to do. I didn't know if this was a trick. Every single one of my actions had consequences beyond me. I knew that. As I wondered whether I should lift my eyes, I thought of the men and women tied to bloody wooden stakes. I saw my family, and I trembled at the thought.

"I said look at me," he barked one more time.

I met his eyes with terror. Like a rabid dog, he could smell it, and that made him happy.

"Do you still feel brave?" The smirk on his face made him look maniacal.

The red scars crossing his skin wrinkled into lumps that looked like tumors breaking out of his face.

"I don't," I replied, and I meant it.

He threw me on the ground with violence. My bones screeched in agony, but I just squinted my eyes as hard as I could.

"We'll see," he said and continued his parade of punishment through the fields.

In the coming weeks, I was beaten regularly. Some days my bones were broken, and I had to be carried by Steve. Other days, it was just a shove that landed me on the ground or a couple of punches that blew the air out of me.

Roman wanted to make sure I understood our deal. He didn't want me to say anything to other slaves. He wanted me to show them what "obedience and servitude" looked like.

Every time a blow hit my body, I would think of my parents and my brother. I needed Roman to know I was holding my end of the bargain. He promised that if I showed obedience, my loved ones wouldn't suffer. The guards were not going to torture me forever, just until the master knew there was no more fight in me.

The human capacity to adapt always fascinated me. From before I arrived at The Mist, I had been amazed at how even the most daring situations could become the new normal for people. A couple of months after Dani lost his legs, things at home had gained a sense of normality. Dad had installed a ramp for Dani's wheelchair. We moved the furniture around to make space for him, and then it felt like we had always lived that way.

After several weeks of constant beatings, I had become accustomed to them. I knew they wanted me to scream, so I did. I also knew they wanted me to beg for mercy, but I didn't. I took every punishment without an ounce of rebellion, but I didn't beg. That piece of me I was not ready to give away.

"Why are they doing this?" Claudia asked me when it became apparent the punishments would continue for a while.

"To make sure I never challenge them again," I replied.

Steve looked at me with pity.

"You are doing the right thing, Andres. Roman told you it would be over as soon as he was convinced you were not a threat. I think that is clear by now."

Claudia's eyes opened like the mouth of a lion about to roar.

"They will not stop until they kill him, Steve. They are just taking their time." She was angry and concerned.

"They won't. When you kill a hero, you create a martyr."

"He is right, Claudia. Those are the exact words Roman used."

"We need to stop this." Claudia was losing her patience.

I agreed with Claudia. The flame of bravery was not completely extinguished inside me. But I was lost. I didn't know how to get my fight back. The fear of losing my family was paralyzing.

CHAPTER 13

Balthazar's soft voice woke me.

"Come with me," he said, holding my hand and signaling to stay quiet.

The world spun into a whirlpool of color, and then I was standing one more time in the hall of the augurs' church.

"I need to go back, Balthazar," I said, panicking. "If you rescue me, they will kill my family."

"I'm not here to rescue you, Andres. I'm here to ask you to stay strong." He kept my hand in his palm. "I know you are afraid. I know you feel hopeless, but you have to remember who you are." He looked at me with pride in his eyes. "You are the worlds walker. You have the power to endure this and so much more. You will inspire a revolution."

I didn't want to be the worlds walker. I was tired of the beatings and scared for my family. What was the point of being this legendary warrior if I couldn't keep those whom I loved safe?

"I can't be your hero, Balthazar. I don't know how to fight back without risking my family or Claudia and Steve. I'm too afraid."

"The path will open in front of you. When the time comes, you will know exactly what to do," he said in his ominous voice.

I was reaching the limit of my patience. "Why don't we stop the riddles and you just tell me what to do."

"Because I don't know what you should do. I just know that this painful path is about to end, but only you can decide how to end it. Until you make a decision, I can't tell what the future holds."

The church was quiet. The scene that night was so different from the first time Balthazar took me there. The slaves were sleeping, and the fireplace was the only light illuminating the place. I wondered if it was also the middle of the night in the human world. I imagined my parents sleeping under a mountain of blankets with the soft sound of the TV in the background. My grandma would be reading, because with age she had lost the will and need to sleep.

"Will my family survive?" I asked. "I need to know if all this suffering is worth it. If I do what Roman wants me to do, will he leave my family alone?"

"He has not decided to kill them. That doesn't mean he won't. It just means he has not made that decision."

I sat on a bench and covered my face with my palms. I wanted to grab Balthazar by his shoulders and shake him until answers started coming out of him. He was an augur. He had the power to see the future. What was the point of his powers if he couldn't guide my decisions?

Since that dreadful night at Tumultuous, my entire existence had depended on Roman's will. For once I wanted to have the advantage. I wanted to be a step ahead. I needed to disentangle my fate from him, but my soul knew that was impossible.

"Roman is the prince of your prophecy, isn't he?" The question had been roaming my brain since our visit to the gallery. I knew the answer. I just hoped Balthazar would tell me I was wrong.

"He is."

"How long have you known?"

"Since the day he was born."

I cried. I couldn't stop myself. Tears started pouring from my eyes because the next question was obvious and so was the answer.

"Are we brothers?"

The augur put his hand on my lap, but I pushed him away. He was not about to numb me from this pain. I wanted to feel every ounce of rage and sadness racing through my veins.

"You both were born from a slave called Ruth. You were separated at birth. He remained in this world. Your father attempted to free you from your destiny by giving you to a human family."

"You lied to me the first time we talked," I accused him.

"It wasn't for me to reveal this truth. Now I'm just confirming what you already knew in your heart."

My entire existence was a lie. The parents I loved were not my real parents. The brothers who tortured me were not my own blood. I wondered how much they all knew about my real nature. I wasn't only a bastard, I was an abomination. The product of a monster and either a rape victim or a whore. That part of the story I didn't need to hear.

"Does he know? Roman. Does he know we are brothers?" My voice got louder.

"No, he doesn't."

We grow up believing we are owners of our destiny. We are told over and over that our choices determine our fate, that we have the power to change our circumstances and forge our future. All those empowering phrases were nothing but bullshit for Roman and me. We were born destined to hate each other. We were never given a choice in the matter. He was declared villain, I was declared hero, and now we had to fight until one of us was dead.

We were not identical. Did that mean we were complementary? Could I do things he couldn't? Had I been blessed with the greater powers, or had he? There were so many questions yet so little space in my brain to hear answers.

"I'm not doing this," I said among sobs. "I'm not fighting him. This is your war and not mine. I will keep my family safe. No matter who I am or what I am, they are still the people I love."

"I'm not asking you to stop caring for them—"

"Take me back," I cut him off.

He didn't say another word. I went back to the slave quarters and lay in my bed with my eyes wide open and my mind blank. The world was crumbling around me, and some old book said I had to fix it. "Swim or sink," I said, remembering the first swimming lesson I received from my brothers.

CHAPTER 14

Balthazar asked me to make a decision, and I did. I was going to convince Roman and Ash they had won. I was going to be submissive and obedient, and when I was sure they believed me, I was going to find a way to escape. The augurs needed to find a new hero. My decision was made; getting my family to safety was my only and final goal.

That morning the guards were as gruff as always. I started my shift moving like a man with a purpose, hoping that maybe that was the day my torture ended. The hours passed, and a twinkle of hope began sparking inside me. Maybe it was over. Maybe I had convinced them that I was no longer a threat.

Roman and Ash appeared at midday. They probably wanted to assess for themselves that I was no longer a hazard. Their presence was hope and doom. It meant the constant punishment was about to end. It also meant this time it would be the most brutal.

As soon as Ash's hand waved at the giants, three of them stomped in my direction.

"You can do it," I mumbled.

The sole of his boot found my stomach. I flew and fell to the ground in pain. Half-digested goo exploded from my guts, tainting the white surface with a nasty green-and-yellow tint.

They were kicking me and yelling at me. The green bile drooling from my mouth started turning red. My brain was fading to black. Every time I returned to my body, a new blow would send me stumbling back into a semiunconscious state.

I heard Claudia's screams, and I panicked. My eyes snapped open, and I tried to warn her to stay away, but another blow stopped my voice. I saw her running toward me, demanding they stop beating me. When the guards' blows slowed down, I knew death was heading her way.

They left me there sprawled like a human scarecrow. I attempted to move, but my limbs weighed me down. They were numb, drained of life by all the blood I had lost.

It took only one fist to her head to knock her out. Then the guards started throwing her body around like a rag doll. Her head hung to the side, and her arms flew lifelessly every time she was airborne. Claudia landed on top of a bed of eilifts; the crystal pricks gored her face, and her blood drenched the soil.

Steve jumped on top of one of the monsters and started hitting him until his knuckles were bleeding. The guard grabbed him as if he were an annoying bug and threw him away without any trouble. Despite the sound of broken bones, Steve got up and charged again, hoping to take the attention away from Claudia.

I forced my extremities to move and crawled my way to where my friends were losing their battle. The enormous figures were not interested in me anymore. They just wanted to kill those two who had dared to interrupt their fun. Blood was pouring from Claudia's and Steve's wounds. It was just a matter of time until life abandoned their bodies.

"Please!" I yelled. "I beg you. Please have mercy on us." I summoned the whispers of breath left in my body and continued. "I swear I will be good. Please spare our lives!"

Their smiles felt like lashes. The sight of their backs walking away from us felt like salvation.

Claudia and Steve lay lifeless. Their faces were distant and pained, like a lost love.

CHAPTER 15

I felt Roman's panic. His thoughts screamed angry and clear like a banshee in the middle of the night. In the midst of the mayhem that ended one of my friend's lives, the twisted sounds of his mind echoed inside me.

It worked both ways. My brother and I were able to walk the hallways of each other's minds as if they were the galleries of a lonesome museum. His thoughts were shouts, but also photographs; some of them were scribbles in memories he was trying to erase.

"Twin telepathy," I said to myself. "What a cruel joke."

The first revelation was that he was worried. I had dipped my fingertips in the murky waters of his thoughts for just a second, but it had been enough to know that Claudia and Steve had ruined his plan. He knew the guards had made a cardinal mistake by killing someone so close to me. My friends jumping to my defense was an unexpected twist, and the bloodthirsty giants reacted the only way they knew how, like savage animals.

I couldn't remember how I'd made it to the butchering room. One moment I was standing in the field—lost is sadness and despair—and the next I was seizing a machete, ready to turn an innocent into food for monsters.

The smell of blood and guts didn't bother me. Death had become so commonplace that my senses were indifferent to its gory and foul aftermath. I looked at the figure in front of me and tried to think of it as just a carcass. The generous soul who had inhabited it was gone. There was no reason to cry over the empty shell lying on the table.

I worked in a trance. My blade slid from one corner of the body to another, with the growls of the fenrirs as background noise. The knots in my chest and my throat kept growing, but I ignored them. My hands shook so hard I had to hold the machete with both of them to keep it steady.

"It is just a corpse. The soul you are mourning is, at last, free." The words flowed from my mouth like a chant. I repeated my mantra over and over while battling the feelings blistering me inside.

I brushed the sweat from my forehead and looked at my work. There was nothing but a pile of bones left.

"The worst part is over," I mumbled.

Chopping the skeleton was my final macabre task. I made an effort to cut through the femur, but it was like sawing through a granite column. The saw's blade struggled with the solid mass until it broke, slicing part of my fingertip in the process.

"Shit!" I put the finger in my mouth and heard the beasts at the bottom of the pit growling. They were getting impatient.

I ripped off a piece of my uniform and wrapped it around my finger. I looked around for another saw, but there were just blades. I either shaved the bones into dust or gave them to the beasts whole.

I sat on the floor with my back against the wall. The stone was colder than I expected, but the chill in my spine woke me up from my numb state. My head rested on my hands. The fenrirs got louder. They were starving, and I was making them wait. I wondered how hungry they had to get before they jumped from their lair to where I was sitting.

I squinted as hard as I could and summoned all my determination. I grabbed the two femurs resting on the table, and as I walked toward the cave's mouth, it dawned on me. Steve's body was our way out of The Mist. His sacrifice would bring freedom to us. A sad but hopeful smile flourished on my face.

"He would have liked that."

I walked into the slave quarters with a plan in my head and two sharp objects tied to my thighs. I couldn't smuggle knives out of the butchering room, but those were not the only weapons available.

As I held Steve's bones, one of the most repulsive memories from my camping trips with my brothers flashed in front of my eyes like an epiphany: once I saw them turn a deer leg into a knife using nothing but rocks.

"You smack the bone with any heavy object until it breaks into many pieces," said Jorge while striking the leftovers of the gentle beast with the force of an earthquake. "Then you pick the sharpest piece, and you shave it with a sharp rock until it looks like a blade."

The scene had grossed me out to the point of vomiting, but not this time. Steve's femurs were sturdy, and it took more than a couple of blows to break them, but when they did, two perfect fragments emerged. I used the machete to turn them into knives and pieces of my belt to attach them to my legs.

Steve was the willing hero the prophecy talked about. He had sacrificed his life to save Claudia's. The moment he decided to jump onto the giant's back, he knew his life was about to end. The weapon that would kill the oppressors had to be forged from his bones.

***

I knew that if I got caught, the guards would kill me, but I had nothing to lose. Death was coming for me. It was just a matter of time until Roman and Ash figured out how to end my life without turning me into the poster child for an uprising.

"You look like crap," I told Claudia and grinned.

"You don't look so hot either." She attempted to smile, but her facial muscles didn't cooperate.

I sat at the end of her bed and stared at the black-and-blue spots disappearing from her arms and her face. The healing water was working its magic.

"Is he dead?" The sadness in her words was as vast as the cruelty in The Mist.

I nodded. Claudia's tears crawled from her eyes like frightened children trying to escape unnoticed. Her chest spasmed as she fought her body's urge to cry. She was holding on to her sobs as if they were her last possession.

"Did you take care of his body?"

"I did."

She smiled and reached for my hand. We sat in silence as we had the evening we were ordered to feed Leo's body to the fenrirs. That moment had changed the course of our destinies. This moment was about to send us onto the next leg of our trip.

"They won't stop, right?" She looked at me, exhausted.

"No, they won't."

"Why are we still alive, then?"

"Because Roman is afraid."

She looked at me in disbelief. "Afraid of us? Of you?"

"He is afraid of what my death may create. He needs to isolate me again so I don't become the spark that ignites the slaves."

She reflected on my statement. I could tell she was deciding if my words made sense or were just ego-infused gibberish.

"What now, then?"

I felt the blades pinching my legs, and for one second, I considered sharing my crazy idea, but I didn't. Claudia needed to mourn. She needed time alone to cry in silence for the death of her best friend. I knew that as soon as I left she would allow herself to sink deeper into the sadness of his loss.

"Now we rest. Tomorrow we'll figure out our next steps," I said, getting up. "Try to sleep, Claudia. We both know tomorrow won't be easy."

***

Her scream echoed with such force every soul in the meadows froze. She was kneeling just a couple of rows ahead of me, holding in her arms the body of a young woman I didn't recognize.

The girl's skin was as white as the fields surrounding her body. Her lips were a transparent shade of pink, and her curly red hair flowed like a hot stream of lava pouring into the dusty ground. The woman holding her was named Amanda.

The likeness of the two women was undeniable. It was just the fading glow of youth that made it clear that they were mother and daughter and not sisters.

Amanda hadn't seen her daughter for many years, but she recognized her face right away. She had dreamed about those freckles every night since becoming a slave. She would talk about her baby to anybody willing to listen.

"Emily! Emily!" she yelled between sobs while clutching the already stiffening body to her chest.

We all looked at her in awe as if she were a haunting spirit forcing us to witness her grief. But the presence of a dead body was not what frightened us. The identity of the dead woman was the terrifying part of that scene. She was not a slave. Emily had been kidnapped from the human world and murdered to send us all a message.

The guards ripped the body out of Amanda's hands and walked away, unconcerned with the mother's cries. Nobody consoled her. We stood frozen, too shocked and too afraid to say or do anything.

That morning the guards had told Amanda in which row she had to work. They wanted her to find the body, and they wanted all of us to see it. The message was loud and clear: it was not about our safety anymore, it was about those we had left behind too. Roman and Ash had just slammed their fists on our chess board and showed us that nobody was safe under their rules.

"Back to work, all of you!" The voice of the guard broke the silence.

Amanda sat there with an empty expression. Her knees were touching each other, and her feet were pointing in opposite directions. The entire weight of her body was resting in the palms of her hands, from where they had ripped her daughter away.

Steve said that the human soul was immortal, but he was wrong. The woman I was watching was nothing but a husk. The essence that made her human was gone. Her lungs were still inhaling, her nails might continue growing, and her tears would never stop pouring, but she was dead. Behind those bloodshot eyes, there was nothing left for the monsters to take.

It happened in a split second. A disfigured giant was walking toward her, ordering her to get up, when she reached for the eilift and slit her throat. Blood splashed the bright flowers around her. A gasp resounded through the land. Even the guard stopped in his tracks, as in shock as everybody else.

The sound of her skull hitting the ground was the eeriest part. A small cloud of dust hovered around the crown of her head like a misplaced halo, and then it was over.

From then on, a new body appeared every day. Early morning screams became a routine that kept everybody in constant terror. It wasn't always someone related to slaves in our barracks, but we were no doubt the favorite subjects for this new form of torture.

The days of standing in line behind your friends were over. Once we got to the fields, we were all scattered. That way nobody would have a clue of who "the chosen one" was that morning. Their plan had been thought out.

Nights at the slave quarters became tense. This new fear birthed desperation, and desperation made feelings of aggression flourish. The mob needed someone to blame, and of course, I was the perfect scapegoat. I had challenged the guards more than once, and slaves had challenged the masters to protect me when I was dying. Steve's and Claudia's actions had been the final straw that drove the oppressors to a new level of cruelty.

Roman had to up his game. Not only he was reminding everybody who was in control, but he was making sure that "pariah" was my permanent status.

The murmurs that followed me wherever I went were the most horrible part of my punishment. It was just a matter of time until someone crossed the line between anger and violence. Somebody would throw that first stone, and then my fellow slaves would do the master's dirty work by killing me. I had to admit it, Roman's plan was brilliant.

"Do you fear for your parents?" Claudia asked with worry in her voice.

"They won't kill my family. At least not yet. They are too clever for that."

"What do you mean?"

"Killing someone I love would make me just another victim of their cruelty. Roman wants the rest of the slaves to hate me so much they wish me to die."

"You seem quite sure of what his plan is." Skepticism marked Claudia's voice.

I didn't answer her. I knew what he was planning. Since that day at the butchering room, our connection had become stronger. At night, I dreamed of places and people I didn't know. Those were his dreams, or maybe his memories. I wasn't sure. What I realized was that he was so obsessed with eliminating me that those thoughts were the loudest inside his brain.

Some days his presence was palpable. I felt his claws tearing through my memories, searching for answers to questions he didn't have. Escaping was a move he was not counting on, and I had to keep it that way.

The loudest thoughts were always those connected to the strongest emotions. At first, the happiness that his attention sparked had opened the door to my mind. Then it was fear, and later hate. I had to free myself from those feelings or, at least, keep them at bay while I was planning our getaway.

I started practicing the meditation techniques that had failed me so many times. This time, though, my survival and my freedom depended on it, so I tried harder. I applied the urgency and the discipline of those who can foresee their demise, but it always felt like walking in a minefield. No matter how hard I tried, I was destined to blow myself to pieces.

One night, while working on controlling my breathing with my eyes closed, the idea of compartmentalizing my plan came to me. I had to think of each piece as an independent task and implement as many as I could out of order. If Roman were able to get a grasp of my thoughts, he would have to piece the puzzle together before he could figure out where I was going.

My first step would be regaining the trust of my comrades. Convincing the slaves not to hate me was something Roman would expect me to do. He would think that was nothing but a natural reaction to their threats and a clear expression of my fear.

Public speaking was not my thing, so I didn't attempt some inspiring and moving *Braveheart*-style speech. I just had to talk one-on-one to as many people as I could. I had to remind them of who the real enemy was.

I thought Malcolm—the maximum authority on gossip in the quarters—would be the perfect place to start.

"You brought this curse on us," the old man with the watery eyes barked at me while refusing to sit and talk.

"No, they did. Their cruelty did," I replied.

"Your foolish actions and the actions of your friends made them do it! Don't you see? This kind of punishment never happened before. Our families were never at risk." His voice was irritated and fearful.

"Do you think that murdering our loved ones never crossed their minds before?"

"They had not done it until you started challenging them." He stopped and faced me.

"Why are you defending them, Malcolm?"

His fist closed tight. "Are you trying to piss me off or get me to forgive you?"

"I don't need your forgiveness. I have done nothing wrong. They did."

He frowned, full of annoyance. "Are you expecting an apology from me, then?"

"I just want you to remember who the enemy is."

He walked away without answering, his steps brisk and angry.

Malcolm had lived in The Mist the longest and enjoyed sharing the history of the place. Of course, he always added a big scoop of his own flavors to every story he told. He was known for spreading rumors as well, so I knew that our exchange would go viral in a matter of hours.

My conversation with him made it clear that winning the battle against fear and mistrust was going to be harder than I thought.

I sat next to Margaret despite her threats. I knew she could "whup my ass," as she said, but I also knew that she was respected, and her support would ripple through many other slaves.

"Look around you, Margaret," I said, pointing to the room around us, making a circle with my finger. "How is this working for you?"

Her lower lip dropped as her expression hardened.

"You're asking for it, kid. Haven't you had enough beatings around here?"

"Answer the question, please. Is this the life you want?"

She shook her head and dried her palm on her chest. "You don't get tired? How much more damage do you need to do before you stop?"

"I haven't done any damage. I have shown you all what they are capable of doing. The fact that our families are in danger is not my fault, it's theirs! The monsters are killing them, not my actions."

She stared at me with all her force. She wanted me to lower my eyes. She expected me to back down because I was about to cross a line few had.

"So what do you want, boy? Do you want to start a revolution? Want us to charge the giants and see if one or two make it through the door, just to get killed in the next hallway?"

"I want you to help me open everybody's eyes. The enemy doesn't sleep in these quarters. The enemy sleeps above us, in a comfortable bed with silk sheets." My voice was firm but warm. My words were coming from my heart.

"You want me to save your ass, that's what you want. You know what's coming for you."

"I don't know what's coming for me, Margaret. I don't know if one of my fellow slaves will kill me in my sleep or if Ash will send his guards to make an example of me. But wouldn't it be sad if all of you ended up doing his dirty work?"

"Leave now, kid"—her eyes were closed and her lips tight—"before I forget you are a grown man and start beating your ass."

She meant every word. Margaret had raised many children before she entered The Mist. Some of them were her own; some of them were orphans she found on the streets of Chicago. She had loved every single one of them, but she was from a time when mothers treated ADHD with the end of a stick and fathers punished insolence with a belt.

Lidia was my final target.

"I know what you're doing, Andres. Malcolm and Margaret have done a good job sharing your conversations with them," she said before I started talking.

"What are they saying?"

"They say you are a stubborn son of a bitch and that you are going to get us all killed."

"I'm not trying to get anybody killed, Lidia. What I want—"

"I know what you want, *mijo*. Believe me, we invented revolutions where I grew up." She sat on her bunk and invited me to join her. "Listen, Andres, I saw enough monsters in our world to know how their minds work. I know this is not your fault, but you need to stop fighting." She rubbed my shoulder with that mix of strength and tenderness that reminded me of my mother. "Even though I've seen oppressed people rise against all odds, I don't believe that is possible in this place . . ."

"Lidia, we can still—"

"No, we can't, Andres. Please stop," she ordered me. "You don't have to worry about me or those who follow me. You are one of us. We have your back, but please stop this nonsense."

I didn't get an encouraging word at the end of any of those conversations. But that wasn't the point. I meant what I had said to Malcolm. I didn't want anyone's forgiveness or pity. What I needed was for them to see beyond their fear, where the face of the real enemy lived.

The bodies didn't stop appearing in the fields, but over time, the target of the slaves' anger changed. My words were seeds that I kept watering over and over by talking to as many people as I could until one or two timid shoots started growing.

It took weeks for the men to stop making fists every time I walked in front of them. But the day arrived when their knuckles relaxed. The nasty words behind my back stopped following me, and even a couple of kind smiles surprised me one evening. Deep down they knew I was right. Our actions did not reduce or increase the evilness of our captors. Believing such a thing did nothing but create a false sense of safety.

***

The day of sacrifices was approaching, and Roman was looking forward to it. He was giddy about the plans he had for the occasion. It was sooner than I expected, but I was becoming skillful at dealing with the impossible. It was time to share my plan with Claudia and hope she was ready to execute it on the next day off.

"You did what!" Her eyes were so big and her pupils so fierce I feared she would jump on top of me and beat me to death.

"Steve would have liked this," I said, trying to sound convincing, but part of me could hear his voice calling me insane.

"You desecrated his body to make knives . . ."

"Instead of feeding them to the fenrirs," I interrupted, with more intensity than I wanted. "Steve is the hero the augurs talked about. These knives were made from the bones of a hero."

She sat on her hands, trying not to give in to the urge to slap me.

"And you want to use those two knives"—her face cringed at the word—"to fight an army of giants." She flashed a skeptical smile.

"No, I want to use those knives to take Roman hostage and make him bring us back to our world."

She bit her lip, attempting to find patience somewhere inside herself.

"Andres, there are so many holes in this ridiculous plan I can't go over all of them without getting angrier. But let me just point out the most basic one: What if you are wrong? What if Steve was not the hero whose bones would defeat our captors?"

I had thought about that, and somehow I knew I was right. Like it or not, I was the worlds walker; I was destined to find the weapon that would free the slaves.

"Just listen to me. The day off is approaching." She tried to reply, but I raised my hand and asked her to wait. "I know it is coming, please trust me. Roman will come here that day, escorted by two guards. We will be waiting for him at the door." I could see her eyes getting ready to roll. "You will get behind him as fast as you can and put your knife on his neck while I keep the guards away from him. Believe me, he will not move, and the guards will not attack if you are threatening to slit his throat. If what the augurs said is true, you could sever his whole head with one stroke."

"Have you ever been in a fight?"

She knew the question would hurt. We had talked about this before. I had shared with her my struggle measuring up to my brothers. But I saw right through her intentions. Claudia wanted to discourage me. She was afraid—and I couldn't blame her—for both of us.

"Roman believes the slaves hate me, so he thinks the time is right to make an example of me by killing me in front of everybody." I paused for a second, not sure how to tell Claudia the second part of his plan. "But first he will kill you and make me watch."

She seemed confused.

"How do you know that, Andres?"

"I can hear his thoughts. At least some of them."

Her first reaction was laughter. But when I didn't laugh, her expression turned into uneasiness.

"You are not joking. You honestly believe you can read his mind."

"I know I can. He can read mine too."

She scratched her forehead and exhaled until she had no more air. When her eyes found me, there was such a mix of emotions it was impossible to predict what words would follow.

"Andres, this is crazy. You can't read his mind. Humans don't have that type of power."

"I do," I replied, but I didn't explain why. I couldn't tell her I was a monster, that Roman and I could hear each other's thoughts because we were brothers.

"It is late, and I need to sleep, Andres. I can't deal with all of this right now. The way I see it, if I choose to believe you, you and I will be dead soon. There is no escaping from here,

Andres, so if all of a sudden you are a psychic and know what Roman is thinking, we are nothing but walking corpses."

Claudia rolled over and faced the wall. Her breathing was agitated, and even though I couldn't see it, I imagined the exasperated grimace on her face.

The next day I asked Margaret, Lidia, and Malcolm to listen to my plan. I didn't tell them I could read Roman's thoughts. I just said I was planning to escape the next day off, and I wanted their advice.

"That is suicide, kid," said Margaret.

I told her about my encounter with the augurs and the uprising they were working on. I also told her about the dagger I had made from Steve's bones. They looked surprised by my revelations, but somehow my story did not ignite the outrage I expected. I was worried about Malcolm's reaction, who not too long ago had accused the augurs of turning women into breeding slaves.

The old man rested his chin on his knuckles, nodded a couple of times, and then asked, "Do you believe them?"

"I do."

He then was lost in thought. His face had the conflicted expression of someone fighting to keep his hope alive in the face of a disheartening reality.

"Even if the hidden people are our allies and those knives you made are the actual magical weapons you want them to be, our chances of overcoming the guards with two knives are slim to none."

"I have to try."

Lidia had been quiet all through the conversation. She was the one with the strategic mind. I hoped she was looking at the big picture and assessing our choices.

"Your plan is ridiculous but not impossible. I mean, if every *if* you are counting on occurred, you may have a chance," she said.

"I need others to help me, though. I can't do it alone."

"You'd better figure out how to do it on your own, *mijo*; your only chance of making it out of here alive is by going solo. The bigger your group, the more chances for a slaughter."

Lidia was right; a massive breakout would attract more attention and end with more casualties. For this strategy to work, it had to be just me and, hopefully, Claudia.

Roman planned his grand finale in two parts. I should have known, but I was too busy hiding my own thoughts to notice he had the last surprise waiting for us.

***

The morning before our day off, Claudia found her mother's lifeless body in the fields. A blanket of eilifts covered the woman from her bare feet all the way to her neck, as if someone had created a crystal casket for her. Blinded by disbelief and grief, Claudia started brushing the flowers away, cutting every inch of her skin in the process. The pain from the lacerations was nothing compared with the agony in her heart. She didn't scream or cry. Her bloody palms moved with fury while her lips repeated words only she could understand.

She grabbed the body with tender care as if any sudden move would break the corpse into pieces. Blood trailed down her arms, creating a light-red stain around the two of them. They looked like a work of art writhing in pain. Claudia's agony was raw but astonishingly contained.

She kissed her mother on the forehead and continued whispering. The words flowing into her mother's ear were full of love and nostalgia. She was also telling her she was sorry, not only for her death but for all the suffering she had caused in her previous life.

The guards marched toward Claudia as they did every morning with other slaves. She handed the body over without resistance, grabbed her basket, and started picking flowers as if it were just another day in the white meadows.

"Drink water!" the guard ordered her. They had instruction. She had to survive until Roman's big finale.

Time crawled under a fog of sorrow thicker than other days. I turned to look at Claudia as many times as I could, just to make sure she was ok. Her demeanor was more stoic than usual. Her head stayed down, and her feet kept moving. She was determined to get through the day with her dignity unbroken.

When we got back to the slave dungeon, she grabbed me right away.

"Tell me your plan again."

"Claudia, I'm so—"

"Let's go over your plan," she cut me off. "Someone has to pay for her death. Either me or them."

CHAPTER 16

The thud of marching boots was like a requiem. Claudia's frown turned into panic, and her eyes grew bigger, looking for an answer she thought I should have. She knew what was happening. Death was rushing in our direction like a hurricane, and there was no way out.

I felt the hard handle of my knife in my palm. That weapon was our only hope to succeed. It wasn't a sword, but it was forged from the bones of a hero who sacrificed himself in the name of love and friendship. I closed my eyes, took a deep breath, and hoped I was right. If my blade cut through the skin of at least one of the guards, maybe the few seconds of surprise would give Claudia a small chance to reach Roman.

"You just need to get to him," I said earlier that morning while we were eating. "Don't worry about me, just get to him and the battle will be over. With a knife to his throat, he'll agree to bring us back to our world. Trust me."

She just nodded. Our task was impossible, but there was no turning back.

Roman knew I was waiting, so he changed his plan at the last minute. Instead of bringing two guards with him, as he'd originally intended, he had an army of twenty. They were going to massacre every slave in the quarters. The tyrants had decided that the best way to eradicate their problem was by slaughtering the entire herd.

The eyes of every man and woman were on us. They could hear the stomping too, and even though they couldn't read Roman's thoughts, they knew the Reaper was coming.

Claudia and I were waiting at the entrance's arch. Our shoulders were pressing against the cold and rough stone as if the structure would crumble if we let it go. I turned around and looked at her one more time.

"We can do this," I said with the conviction of a survivor.

"Andres, we thought facing two guards was going to be hard. How are we going to fight an army?" Her voice trembled.

Claudia was the strongest person I had ever met, but even her faith and resilience had a limit.

"I know we have a one-in-a-million chance of succeeding, but one is all we need. They don't know we can hurt them. That gives us the advantage."

She cleared her throat and took a deep breath. Her eyes focused on the knife attached to her hand. She was thinking of Steve. The soft smile on her face told me she heard his deep, cranky voice warning her against following my insane ideas.

"I knew you would be the death of me." She smirked.

"We are not dead yet, Claudia." I held her face with my cold, sweaty palm. "We will get through this. I know it looks impossible, but I know we are destined to win."

"Your hands are gross," she replied, trying to lighten the mood.

They entered the dungeon with the ferocity of a swarm of locusts. At least ten of them had passed in front of me before my knife sliced through the skin of one of the giants. His shriek paralyzed every soul in the room.

The blade cut through the side of his torso as if it were hot wax. There was a slight hint of resistance, but once the sharp object penetrated the first layer, it slid all the way to his back. His serpent eyes cursed me with a death wish. Hatred emanated from them like a vibration I could almost hear. Then there was fear and the sound of his internal organs hitting the floor in a wet, noisy splash.

It had worked. Claudia and I had the only weapons that could hurt our enemies.

I charged toward Roman, who was flanked by two giants. My arm swung with ferocity, mercilessly cutting anything that crossed my path. A blast of hope raced through my veins as I saw the surprise in his expression.

I'm coming for you, I thought loudly, and I knew he could hear it.

Then a fist—unbreakable as a rock and committed as the soldier behind it—sent me flying against a wall. My head hit the stone so hard I felt my brain shaking inside my skull.

It took a couple of seconds for the scene to regain focus, but when it did, my jaw and my heart dropped. There were bodies and blood everywhere. The guards were crushing slaves as if they were bugs running panicked inside a terrarium.

The giant who knocked me down started running toward me. I used the seconds that I had to look for Claudia, but I couldn't see her. I jumped to my feet, made sure the wall was protecting my back, and leaned forward with my knife, wavering like a cobra. He was not scared. My challenge was an invitation he was glad to accept.

The hand holding the blade was so tight that my knuckles were ready to pop right out of my skin. I was prepared to kill him or die trying. The anger and frustration of all those months erupted inside me with the force of a cataclysm. I didn't just want him dead. I wanted him to feel every second of pain in the process.

You are the worlds walker. You have the power to endure this and so much more. The words of the augur repeated, clear and enlightening, in my head, and I prayed he was right.

Two other guards joined the one gunning for me. A wall of muscles and wrath was speeding in my direction, and I knew then my chances of surviving were almost none. I looked at Steve's bone in my hand. Killing the giants and finding a way back to my world was not the only path to freedom. I was not about to let them finish me. Taking control of my own death was freedom too.

I won't give you the pleasure, Roman, I thought with all the intensity I could muster.

I pushed the blade against my throat, and with my eyes fixed on the approaching giants, I got ready to cut and let my life gush away.

The first drop of blood had rolled down my neck already when Balthazar's hand stopped me. My skin shivered with his sudden presence.

"Find the catcher before he escapes," said the augur.

"What are you—"

"Find the catcher!" he yelled and leaped toward the guards. War cries burst from his mouth like an ancient tribal song. There were at least fifty of them entangled in a fierce battle with the monstrous giants.

I saw Roman running toward the entrance. I sprinted behind him as fast as I could, dodging bodies and guts spread on the floor.

The smell of a massacre covered every inch of the chamber. There were so many corpses on the floor it was possible that every single slave was dead already.

"They did it, not you," I repeated, trying to contain the feeling of guilt and the urge to cry for all those innocent souls.

Roman reached the stairs, and then he was out of my sight. If he got to the hallway, finding him before he got reinforcement would be impossible. I sped up. I ignored the muscles burning in my legs and widened my stride, hoping to reduce the distance between us.

My confidence was fading as the entrance seemed to get farther away from me. I was about to give in to the voice in my head telling me there was no point to keep on running when I saw Roman's striking figure walking back into the room. Behind him was Claudia. The blade of her knife rested firmly on the back of his neck. We had the "king."

"Checkmate, asshole," I said, looking straight into his eyes.

His guards stopped fighting as soon as they saw him reenter the room. The army of augurs rushed to restrain the giants. They knew the beasts would not risk getting Roman killed.

Roman wore the expression of someone unimpressed by a disappointing performance. There was no fear in his eyes. His thoughts were loud and infuriating—he knew he had a huge bargaining chip. He was the key.

I wanted to push my knife as deeply as I could into Roman's heart, but he was right; he had to stay alive at least until we were safe.

"You'll never be safe, Andres," he said with a cocky smirk. "If you think this cheap stunt will get you what you want, you are even more stupid than I expected."

He was taunting me, maybe buying time while he figured a way out of his dilemma.

"Take us back."

"I can't." His smile showed triumph.

I put my blade right under one of his eye sockets.

"I can't kill you, but I can make you suffer until you reconsider your stubbornness, Roman."

He flinched. I had surprised him once again.

"I'm not lying. I'm not an augur! I can't just vanish like a damn ghost. I need to open a portal."

I concentrated on his pupils, trying to find the part of his brain that separated truth from lies.

"So it works both ways," he said while shaking his head. "That is why you knew I was coming today." He laughed as if someone had just told him the funniest joke ever. "Isn't this amusing? You, filthy animal, can read my thoughts."

I felt exposed. I didn't know what to say. Did it matter that he or anybody else knew? There was one truth that I certainly didn't want him to know—the fact that we were brothers—but of course, I couldn't stop thinking about it.

"Did you do this?" he pointed with his chin to the augur in front of him.

"We don't possess that kind of power," the seer replied with a stern look.

Roman seemed perplexed. He looked at me with his head tilted and his eyes squinted. Then he smiled.

"You have become quite skillful at blocking me from your thoughts, Andres." He was honestly amused by the situation. "You are a fascinating animal, I knew it from the moment I met you." Roman's voice was soft, even honest, if that was possible for a creature like him.

"Why can't you open a portal here?"

Hearing the firmness and conviction of Claudia's voice made me happy.

"I need a door, an actual door, and a place where the veil between the two worlds is thin."

Claudia and I looked at the augurs, waiting for confirmation.

"He is telling the truth."

My plan didn't include wandering the hallways of The Mist searching for a door. Walking around the castle was dangerous, and since Roman was the only one who knew which door was the right one, he would have plenty of chances to lead us into a trap.

"Then let's go. There is no point in standing here," Claudia said.

"What about them?" I pointed at the few slaves remaining.

"We will take the survivors with us," Balthazar interjected. Then he closed his eyes and paused for a couple of seconds as if he were trying to remember a speech he had practiced before. "I know you want me to come with you, but this journey is yours to complete, Andres."

"We need your help, Balthazar. What if we run into more guards?"

"We can't intervene," he answered. "We can't risk interfering with your fate. Many lives depend on the decisions you will be making, Andres. Be wise. Remember that the catcher has a quick tongue, and he will use it to confuse you." The advice was welcome but unnecessary. I was more than aware of the power of his words.

There was no point in arguing. They had a higher purpose and the power to see the threads of destiny weaving the future. They had made up their minds. For a reason they were not ready to share, Claudia and I had to travel alone with the devil.

Balthazar grabbed my hand, and I felt as if I had just woken up from a restful night of sleep.

"Darkness is your gift, Andres. Walk through the dark path, and you will find the enlightenment you seek."

My head was clear and my determination was unwavering. We were leaving The Mist no matter what.

We walked, slow and alert. Both of our knives were on Roman, but he didn't seem bothered by it.

The central hallway was empty and silent. All its regular inhabitants were witnessing the offerings, rejoicing with the spectacle and the promise of eternal life. Our steps echoed like water drops in a cavern. The longer we walked, the more desolate the scene seemed. It was as if the world had ended and the three of us were the lone survivors.

"How far are we?" Claudia asked.

Roman looked at her with a dismissive grimace. He was not going to make it easy for us.

She pressed the blade harder into his back. "How far are we?"

"Control your girlfriend, Andres, or she'll kill me by mistake and leave you stranded. You are aware I am your way out of this labyrinth, aren't you?" He knew where he stood, and he thought he was in control.

Claudia stepped in front of him, and with one stroke, her blade split his cheek in two. It wasn't a deep cut, but he cried like a wounded dog and pushed her away, making her stumble until she fell. My knife jumped to his throat. Roman froze. His hand covered his face.

"How far?" she asked again while getting up.

"You'll never make it." His voice was blazing with hate.

"I can split your face in two, Roman. How far?" She meant every word, and he knew it.

"Just a little further down. At the end of this hallway, there is a set of stairs; at the bottom there is a door that will open into your world."

"Is he telling the truth?" Claudia asked me. Something in her tone revealed she was looking for an excuse to hurt him more.

"He is." I could sense it.

We continued our passage through the magnificent castle. Ulda's eyes followed us from every picture. Her cruel expressions seemed ominous as the oppressive sense of danger continued to build.

We had been walking for a while when the smell of a banquet surprised us. The sweet perfume of grilled meat danced in front of our noses.

"We can stop for a bite if you want," said Roman. "Nobody is there. I'm sure it'll be ok."

"Where is everybody? Don't you think this is odd?" Claudia asked.

Don't say a word! I thought, and I shoved my knife in Roman's back.

"It is a day of celebration . . . ," he started saying.

The tip of my blade went deeper into his skin.

He looked over his shoulder and found my eyes.

"You're not curious as to why we can read each other's thoughts?" he said with sincere interest.

"No, I'm not."

"Liar."

"Shut up and walk, Roman. This is not a friendly stroll."

"Maybe you are a human seer. Despite popular belief and bad reality TV shows, some of them are real."

He suspected I knew the truth, and he was pushing me to reveal it. Roman was smart and intuitive; deceiving him was not an easy task. "I am not a seer, Roman. For some ridiculous reason, you and I are linked. I'm sure by the twisted will of some cruel joker," I answered, and it wasn't a complete lie. "But it doesn't matter. All that matters is that I can tell when you are lying, and that will get us out of here."

"This place will follow you wherever you go, Andres." For the first time, he was not using the mocking tone I was so accustomed to hearing. "The Mist is now a fragment of your soul, a piece of the machinery that makes you tick. The scars in your soul will never fade. Every time you dare to forget, that nagging feeling of its presence, the memories, will come back to haunt you. The souls of those you killed and those you left behind will haunt you."

"Shut up, Roman!" Claudia was reaching her limit.

"Not a fan of the truth, sweetheart?" He bit his lip and smiled. "You are a smart girl. You don't need his silly power to know what I'm saying is true."

"Can we cut his tongue?" Claudia was dead serious.

"Let's just keep walking . . . in silence, Roman," I ordered.

I didn't know what our next step would be if we were able to leave The Mist. It wasn't like we could run to the authorities and tell them our story. I wasn't even sure if we could warn our families of the danger threatening their lives. How could we protect our loved ones without giving them a reason to institutionalize us? And how long until a group of catchers barged into my parents' house after they realized Roman was missing?

"They will be dead before you can reach a phone and try to warn them." Roman enjoyed answering my thoughts when he noticed my weakness.

The vast hall became smaller as we approached the end. The walls and the ceiling were closing in, almost as if they were shrinking as we walked. The light radiating from the chandeliers was dimmer as well. By the time we reached the bottom of the stairs, the chamber where we stood looked like any ordinary castle in the human world.

That was what Roman meant by the veil between the worlds becoming thinner. Magic seemed weaker in that spot. Even my ability to read Roman's thoughts seemed diminished.

We had not encountered one person on our long trek to the final door. I knew that most of our captors were witnessing the genocide in the fields, but still the solitude was eerie and concerning. I could tell Claudia was thinking the same thing.

"If this is a trap, we kill him before we die," she said, looking at him.

I nodded. "Grab his wrist and keep your grasp on the knife firm. We all make it, or we all die."

"You are so damn dramatic, Andres. The only thing worse than listening to your speeches is roaming your pathetic and insecure brain." Roman's head and eyes rolled back.

"Let's cross," I said to Roman and thrust him forward.

"Your wish is my command, Master." The sense of victory in his wicked smile had my heart pounding.

We felt the heavy stare of all eyes landing on us as soon as we crossed the threshold. Roman's laughter stabbed my ear-drums like a needle as my eyes adjusted to the blinding light. I didn't need my sight to know where he had taken us. We were in the eilift fields.

The wooden stakes holding naked bodies extended in front of us like a vision of a mass witch-burning ceremony. Their wails were as disheartening and as deafening as the first time I had heard them. The faces of the victims were a distorted reflection of the nightmares torturing their brains.

Claudia was shaking. Her mouth was attempting to move, but shock and terror didn't let her articulate a word. Her breathing got quicker and louder. She was fighting the panic, but she was losing the battle.

The women feeding the victims were gone. The fenrirs were coming. I had to get us out of there as fast as possible.

"What is this?" Claudia's voice crumbled.

"There is no time, Claudia. We need to get out of here, or we'll die."

"You've seen this before?" she said in an accusatory manner.

"Of course he has, sweetheart. I invited him to a VIP view-ing. We had a blast." Roman didn't seem concerned by Claudia's mounting rage.

"Take us out of here, Roman. This is your last chance." I put the tip of my blade under his chin.

"You don't get it, do you?" he pouted in a sarcastic way. "I'd rather die than give you what you want. I hate you that much." His face moved right in front of me, the spicy perfume of his breath blowing into my nostrils. "So go ahead, Andres, you and your bitch can slice me into pieces because we are all dying here, no matter what you do."

I heard the roar of the beasts rolling down the hill. They were hungry and furious. Claudia looked at me, expecting an answer I didn't have. Without moving my blade, I attempted to open the door, but it was locked. We not only had to find a different way out, but we had to outrun the fenrirs.

I darted toward the bottom of the hill, pushing Roman with my knife. He didn't resist. He was enjoying my weak attempt to save our lives.

"Don't let him go, he is still our ticket out!" I yelled over my shoulder.

Claudia nodded. There was terror stamped all over her face.

The growls were getting closer. The foul smell of the monsters was traveling ahead of them. It was just a matter of time until their fangs pierced through our flesh and ended our mission. I didn't lift my eyes, but I could hear the crowd cheering. We were a bonus to the show they had come to see.

I knew the eilift field well. I had spent enough time harvesting flowers to learn where every single entrance was. I didn't know if every door was a thinning between the worlds, but I was willing to take my chances.

We raced along the perimeter of the wall heading toward one of the entrances that led to the slave quarters. The next door was just a couple of feet away.

"It will be locked!" Roman's cheerful voice made me want to slit his throat right then and there.

He was right. I pulled with all the strength I had left, but it wouldn't open.

"Open it!" I shouted at him.

The enormous fangs of the fenrirs were flying toward us. Their eyes filled with rage and starvation. The sound of our breaking bones was about to join the cries of those whose bodies the beasts were devouring without mercy.

A black aura started framing my vision. I felt the world fading around me. I was about to pass out.

"Open the door and cross us! You don't want to die like this, Roman."

"Go fuck yourself, Andres." His laugh shattered the already-cracked lining of my emotional stability.

A final surge of strength exploded from my fast-beating heart. I grabbed his arm, raised my knife, and let it fall on his wrist with the might of a Nordic god. The blade didn't find any resistance in his skin and cut clean all the way to the other side. His hand hit the snowy ground with a muted noise. Blood started pouring from his stump with the same ferocity of his screams.

"Cross us!" I shouted once again.

When I looked back, two fenrirs were already suspended in the air, their jaws ready to break us with just one bite. I reached for Claudia's hand.

"I'm so sorry. I am so sorry," I said, and then darkness swallowed us.

CHAPTER 17

The putrid smell of decaying food overwhelmed my senses. I started gagging. Bile erupted from my mouth with violence. The sour taste was all over. I was vomiting and spitting at the same time. But I was alive.

Before I opened my eyes, I heard it. It was the muffled sound of traffic; engines were roaring close by. The rest of the noises started pouring in one by one. I heard sirens and chattering. I heard music and even the subtle buzzing of streetlights.

Claudia was just a couple of feet away from me, attempting to stand up. I rushed to her side and held her shoulders. She smiled. There was so much happiness in her eyes I thought she would kiss me.

"Where is he?" she asked.

I turned around and saw Roman leaning against a wall. A bloody piece of fabric was covering the place where I had severed his hand. He seemed as disoriented as we were.

I recognized the place. The fluorescent light, the metal door, the Dumpster at the end of the alley. We were where everything had started.

I rushed to grab my knife and pointed it at Roman. He was at least ten feet away from us, but I was not about to take chances.

"So you were not as ready to die as you bragged?" I yelled, feeling full of confidence.

I had called his bluff, and he had folded. We were back in Queens.

He stared at me with a grimace of disgust. I didn't need to read his mind to know how angry he was. If the pain he was feeling weren't so intense and if he weren't as afraid of my knife as he was, he would have torn me to pieces with his bare hands.

I knew I couldn't stop him if he decided to open the door and go back to his world. I wasn't close enough, and I was also exhausted.

"Brothers." Roman spit the words as if they were poison. In the confusion of our escape, I had lowered my guard and given him a full view of my thoughts.

I felt Claudia's eyes on me. I couldn't look at her yet. I wasn't ready.

"That doesn't mean anything, Roman," I shouted. "You go your way and I go mine. We can end this right here."

We stood there gawking at each other like feral animals, waiting for an excuse to attack.

"And you cut my fucking hand," he said, recriminating. As if I owed him any kind of deference or respect.

"I had to do it, Roman. I figured inflicting excruciating pain on you was my last chance of making you cross us back to this world." I swallowed so much saliva it hurt my throat. "I just did what I had to, and it worked."

"No, it didn't work, moron. I didn't open a portal—you did!"

I heard every part of his sentence, but I couldn't understand what he was saying. Words had lost their meaning.

"You don't need to lie or try to trick me anymore, Roman. You know I can't stop you from leaving, and you know you can't stop us. The game is over . . . at least for now."

He let out an exasperated sigh. "I didn't open the door, Andres. Even if I had changed my mind, it was too late." He looked away from me and then continued. "You disgusting mutt, you somehow opened a portal out of thin air and dragged us all back here!" The muscles in his face tensed—the pain was getting worse. "Think about it. We are back to the one place where you know there is a door. I know thousands of doors, and believe me, if I had my choosing, we would have ended far from here, not at your doorstep." His voice was getting louder.

The truth opened in front of me, clear and empowering. "I'm the worlds walker. I can walk between worlds," I said more to myself than in answer to Roman's accusation.

"The augurs knew it." He clenched his jaw. "That is why they orchestrated this ridiculous escape plan. They needed to trigger you. They knew this would happen."

"If they knew I could cross between worlds, why not tell me? I could have saved myself and others from that bloodbath if they taught me how to do it."

"You have no idea who your trusted augurs are. They don't care about you or your kind, Andres. They will never free the slaves, because they need soldiers. They need fools willing to die while they take over." His back collapsed harder into the wall. He was hurting.

Roman was about to speak again when the red-and-blue lights surprised us. Two police officers were running toward us, ordering us to drop our weapons and raise our hands. Their guns were pointed at us already.

Claudia and I looked like junkies. Blood covered our clothing, I had a knife in my hand, and I was threatening a man with a missing hand. They didn't need an excuse to shoot us.

I dropped my knife and turned around to face them. I heard the door slamming on my back as soon as I took my eyes away from it. Roman was gone.

The police pushed us against the wall. My cheekbone slammed into the concrete, but I didn't even feel it. Claudia and I were facing each other.

"We'll be ok," she whispered.

"Where is the other one?" the man in the uniform yelled.

"He is back in hell." I closed my eyes and ground my teeth. "He's back in hell."

ACKNOWLEDGMENTS

Thank you to the following people whose contributions and support made it possible for this book to be written and published:

A mis padres, Ruth y Ricardo, por celebrar cada una de las palabras que he escrito. Sin su constante aliento y amor, nunca me habría atrevido a contar las historias que llevo dentro.

Koleen Kaffan, for giving me the confidence to tell this story and editing with relentless fury.

The Urrutia family, for adopting me when I was alone and celebrating my accomplishments as if I were your blood.

The Donato family, because without your love and trust, I would have never made it in this country.

The GOB—Julie Freddino, Amanda Vercellone, and Kelly Burns—for your unconditional love, for the constant laughs, and for not judging me when I needed no judgment.

Mandi Jackson, because you will never know how many times you saved my life by asking me to grab a coffee.

My friends and colleagues at United Way, for jumping into the crazy train without questions and riding it until *The Catcher's Trap* hit funding.

The Inkshares team, for an unexpected and life-changing opportunity.

The Doctor, because everything I know about the universe, I learned from you. I'll keep waiting for you, Doctor.

ABOUT THE AUTHOR

Ricardo Henriquez was born in the small fishing and mining town of Tocopilla, Chile. He received a degree in journalism from the Universidad Católica del Norte and worked as a political journalist for six years before immigrating to the United States in 2001. For five years he served as a political and community organizer in New Haven, Connecticut. His experiences working with those lacking hope and resources have inspired some of the characters in his writing.

Henriquez has fifteen years of experience writing columns for local newspapers, starting blogs, and sharing his thoughts on social media. He currently lives in Connecticut with his husband, Tom, and their dog, Penny-Lane. When he's not writing, he works at a nonprofit that helps families become financially stable. *The Catcher's Trap* is his first novel.

LIST OF PATRONS

This book was made possible in part by the following grand patrons who preordered the book on inkshares.com. Thank you.

Amy Barrett
Amy O'Connor
Betty Rose Barsa
Bill Burns
Brandon Moore
Brian Guthrie
Christopher B
Danielle Barrett
Dave Barrett
Fedor Urrutia
Jake Tuite
James K. Falconer
Janna Grace
Jeremy Thomas
Johanna D. Robles
Julie Freddino

Kimberly Pisani
Kizel Urrutia Moore
Koleen Kaffan
Leanne Phillips
Luis Aviles
Maria Perez Andrade
Meredith Douglass Berger
Michael F. Walsh
Ricardo A. Henriquez
Ruth Campos
Sandy Schiff
Vicki Suslovic

INKSHARES

 Inkshares is a crowdfunded book publisher. We democratize publishing by having readers select the books we publish—we edit, design, print, distribute, and market any book that meets a preorder threshold.

Interested in making a book idea come to life? Visit inkshares .com to find new book projects or start your own.